PURSUIT
IN
OCEAN PINES

PURSUIT
IN OCEAN PINES

BY DANA PHIPPS

Palmetto Publishing Group
Charleston, SC

Pursuit in Ocean Pines

First Edition

Printed in the United States

ISBN-13: 978-1-64111-401-1
ISBN-10: 1-64111-401-0

Hearts can break and never mend together

Love can fade away

Hearts could cry when love won't stay forever

Hearts can be that way

Song by Mary Balin

Songwriter Jessie Neal Barish

Hearts lyrics Shapiro Bernstein & Co. Inc., The

Bicycle Music Company

To my whole wonderful family

C HAPTER 1

May 4, 2015

Some people have all the luck. Amie McCombe's friends think that of her. She was a young and beautiful woman. Amie and her husband, Patrick, had been married a year and lived in a newly built home in Ocean Pines that, incredibly, she won from a raffle held yearly by the community's fire department. Amie and Patrick's custom-designed rancher was the perfect size for the newlyweds and had a view of Assawoman Bay, which overlooked the Ocean City, Maryland, skyline from their sunroom. The bay, located between Ocean City and mainland Delmarva, was considered a lagoon and was anywhere from two to twenty feet deep.

Ocean Pines was a favorite haven for retirees and families with kids, and it made a wonderful vacation spot for tourists to visit in the summer, especially since it was so close to the bay and Atlantic Ocean. Most everything you could possibly want to do was right there. The McCombes loved living in a wooded and waterfront community.

Amie kept her lightly bleached hair shoulder length and her tanned, lithe body fit. Patrick was toned, strapping, and handsome. Amie couldn't have been happier the past year being with Patrick in their new surroundings…until one warm May morning.

The seventy-six-degree May day called for a sleeveless dress, which Amie slipped on for work. Her stomach sank when she opened her front door to leave and saw who was standing on her front lawn. Her ex-boyfriend, Paul Simmons, stood motionless on the grass, eyes fixed on her house. No words passed between them, and Amie watched him abruptly turn around, get into his black Ford truck, and speed away.

Why was he here? How odd seeing him in front of my house. Haven't seen him since 2010. What the heck did he want? Surely Paul has moved on with his life. Does he know I've married Patrick? How did he find my address?

She headed to work at Cathell Realty, her stomach queasy.

Patrick McCombe was late coming home. He sighed heavily, plopped down on the sofa, and rested his head back on the soft pillow. He heard oil hissing in the kitchen. "Amie, stop whatever you're doing in there. Don't bother to fix dinner. You want to order carryout from Southgate Grill?"

In the kitchen, Amie finished drying her hands on the tea towel. As she poked her head out of the kitchen, she said, "You know, I think I do, honey. I didn't realize I was out of minced garlic, and I need it for this recipe I'm making. So I'm all for getting carryout. I showed two houses today and had an unusually late settlement. I'm beat anyway. You must be too."

"Yeah, I had a tough day. My latest assignment kept me busy and is turning out to be a bit more complicated than I realized. In Milford, Delaware, I was tailing a possible cheating husband in a white Chevrolet Cobalt to a building that advertised window blinds. From a distance, in the rear of the place, the guy looked like he could have been distributing drugs to two other men, and he had a gun tucked in the waistband of his jeans. It looked like he received cash from the men and stuffed it into a bag."

Patrick took a deep breath and shook his head. "I'll have to have Crabbe help me out with this one and get the police involved too."

"I don't like the sounds of this case," Amie said. "Could be dangerous. Maybe you should think about getting out of the private-eye business, but I'm glad Crabbe is now working with you after his retirement from the Ocean Pines Police Department. Be careful, please."

"Don't worry," he said. "I'll be very careful."

She sat down next to Patrick on the sofa. "Guess what happened this morning? Really weird. As I was leaving for work, Paul Simmons was right there next to our mailbox, staring straight ahead at our house. When I opened the front door, he turned around and drove off in his truck."

"That's a bit interesting. After all these years, he suddenly appears at your house? Maybe he heard you won the house raffle and was curious to see the home you won. Who knows? Maybe he's pining for you. Let me know if you encounter him again," said Patrick.

"I doubt if he's pining for me, though it was unsettling. I haven't seen him in eons. It's been about five years. He hasn't been in touch with me since we broke up. After two years with him, I didn't want to continue our relationship. Remember I told you he lived with this mother? Sometimes he invited her to dinner when we went out, and he also brought her to the movies with us once. I thought it was sweet of him, but on the other hand, he did have some peculiar mannerisms."

"Sounds like a mama's boy. Wonder if he still lives with her," said Patrick.

"I wouldn't be surprised. I think she wanted Paul and me to get married. He was one of those people who unfortunately got under my skin at times. Paul was persistent and liked doing things his way, sometimes going through the roof with his demands. He hated that I worked at night. There was never any compromise between us. He pursued interests I didn't care for, and vice versa. We became less and less compatible. When we were dating, a fraternity brother of his at the university told me they had nicknamed him 'Crackers' because of some of the screwy things he did. But I never did ask him what kinds of things they were."

Patrick laughed and said, "Enough about Paul. Let's order dinner."

⚏

On Saturday, May 9, Amie scheduled an open house on the Wood Duck Canal in Ocean Pines, three blocks from where she and Patrick lived. She opened the lockbox, walked into the kitchen, and placed her purse next to the refrigerator. She went outside to post the sign: OPEN HOUSE 2:00 p.m. to 4:00 p.m. The canal house was a real gem and showed well after Amie had staged it. The owners respected Amie and followed her advice to declutter their bathrooms of all their notions as well as power wash their deck. Amie double-checked and glanced around the first floor. She took a deep breath. *Looks ready. Should generate lots of interest.*

After moseying up the sidewalk, several couples came inside, and Amie welcomed them.

They veered off in different directions, whispering to one another about the house. One pair was especially interested in the house.

"Pretty nice view up and down the canal," the husband said. "We have a Jet Ski that would be perfect for that boat lift out back, and it has easy access to deep water."

"But there's no garage," said his wife.

"I like that it has new appliances, a gas fireplace, and tons of storage." He turned to his wife and smiled. "I know you'll like decorating it," he said.

Amie scribbled down their names and scheduled an appointment for them the next day to see the house again. Since so many people had gathered on the outside deck and congregated in the rooms of the house, the retired couple couldn't really observe everything in detail and talk to Amie in private.

At 4:20 p.m. Amie headed to the front door to remove the open-house sign. As she entered the living room, her stomach sank again, and her eyes opened wide. Paul stood there in the middle of the room, taking notice of the surroundings. "Oh, you scared me," Amie said, catching her breath and placing her hand over her heart.

"Well, well, look who's here," said Paul. "You haven't changed a bit. Still as gorgeous as ever, with your long, blond hair and that fine, curvy figure," he said as he eyeballed her up and down.

Amie looked away awkwardly and didn't smile. "What's going on, Paul?" *I know he saw my name on the realtor sign.* "I saw you outside my house the other day, and now you're here." She felt her heart thumping.

"I'm looking to buy a house in Ocean Pines. Yesterday, I was driving around the community observing houses on the water that were for sale. Maybe that's why you saw me. And that's why I'm here at the open house today."

Amie stared at him, her thoughts nagging her. *You were standing in front of my house yesterday. Give me a break. There were no for sale signs on my street.* "Paul—"

He quickly said, "My mom passed away several months ago, and I wanted to move away from Salisbury. I sold her house. Too many memories."

"Oh, I'm so sorry, Paul." Amie shook her head and paused. "She was a lovely person. I liked her a lot. I had no idea she passed away."

"Well, she wasn't in the best of health. The stroke took its toll on her."

"Again, I'm sad to hear that. I could talk more, but Paul, I'm about to close up. I have another appointment. I can show it to you another time if you like." *I wish he'd leave.*

"You mean to tell me you can't show me the house right now? I'd like to catch up on things with you. Haven't seen you in a long time. Aren't you interested in hearing about what I've been up to after all this time?"

Not really. Can't have a normal and comfortable conversation. The back of Amie's neck was tingling. Her heart was pumping faster. Looking at her watch, she said, "No, I'm sorry. I can't. As I mentioned before, I have to be somewhere else, and I would be late if I showed it to you now. Here's my card, and let me know when you can come back," she said, trying hard not to be mean.

Paul's eyes narrowed, and he stared hard at Amie. "OK, suit yourself," he said. He grabbed her business card and gave her his. "We should meet for lunch. You probably will be showing me a lot of houses in the area. I'm picky," he said, grinning.

Amie said, "Sure. You know how to get in touch with me." *Hope he doesn't call me on my cell phone.* Amie winced as she saw him licking his lips.

Paul smoothed his coffee-brown hair, winked at Amie, put on his Ray-Ban sunglasses, and strutted out the front door. She had not faced him, cringing instead. Amie slipped her phone inside her purse and secured the lockbox. She watched Paul leave and then removed the open-house sign outside. *What a relief he's gone. Have to tell Patrick I saw him again.*

Monday, May 11, Amie's cell phone buzzed inside her purse while she was getting ready to head out to Walmart. She withdrew her phone. "Hi, gorgeous. It's me, Paul. When can you show me that house on that canal?"

Amie said, "Oh, no. I'm sorry, Paul. A retired couple signed the contract for it the day after the open house."

"Are you kidding me? Why didn't you call me? You knew I was interested in it," said Paul.

"It sold real fast. They actually saw it before you did. It was a great house," said Amie.

"How much did they pay for it? Would the owners accept another contract over what the retired couple paid for it?"

"No, it's a done deal, Paul," said Amie.

"Well, I'm disappointed you didn't contact me...seeing how we were once very close."

"You have to move fast on the good ones," said Amie. She swallowed hard.

"How about if we have lunch?" asked Paul.

"I can't Paul. I'm heading to Walmart, and I'm married now. I don't think that's a good idea."

Paul clicked off the phone. Amie shrugged. *Good riddance. Hope that's the end of it.*

Amie headed to her best friend Cici's salmon-colored condo building in Marina Cove. She dialed Cici's number on the way over so she could wait out front. Amie saw her come out of the elevator and walk toward the parking lot. Amie thought she looked like a different woman after the ordeal she had endured two years ago with her crazy, now-deceased ex-husband, Greg. *Shouldn't think ill of the dead. But Greg was an exception to that belief, so I don't feel one bit guilty speaking ill of him.*

Cici looked attractive in a dress that hugged her tightly. Her green eyes sparkled when she saw Amie. She waved, and Amie drove to a spot where Cici could get into the car. "I hope the sale at Walmart is a good one," Cici said as she opened the car door.

"OK. Buckle up. I want you to look at a patio set I've had my eye on for the pool deck. The lounge chairs in the set I have now are rusty, and the fabric is ripped on two of them. I'd like your opinion of the set I want to buy," said Amie.

"Sure, and I want to get a few potted palms for my patio anyway," said Cici.

"Why are you going to do that now? Your lease is almost up, right?" asked Amie.

"Yes, but I can lug the plants with me to Joe's new house. They'll look nice on his outside deck. I guess I should say *our* outside deck."

"Who would have thought that you and Joe would end up together, and he and Patrick would be partners at Discovery Investigations? And we all would live in Ocean Pines?" said Amie.

"I agree," said Cici.

"Finally we both have two great guys. They rock!" said Amie. "You won't believe this, but guess what? Paul, my old weirdo boyfriend, wants to move here to Ocean Pines."

"Really?" said Cici. "How do you know that? Did you see him? Does he still look the same?"

"He came to my open house over the weekend. He's still well built and wears his slick hair back and neatly combed. He must have spent a load on getting his teeth whitened. They're gleaming now." Cici laughed. "What I don't like is how he gawks at me with those deep-set smoky, gray eyes of his," said Amie. "He still makes patronizing and snide remarks that make me feel uneasy and off balance. He hasn't changed at all."

Cici asked, "Is he married?"

"I have no idea," Amie said.

The girls entered Walmart and each grabbed a shopping cart. "I have to go to the restroom first, Cici," said Amie.

"I'll look at birthday cards while you're in the bathroom. Meet you by the card section," said Cici.

Amie walked into the restroom and had no trouble finding a stall, since she was the only person in the bathroom. She built her toilet paper nest, neatly arranging it on top of the seat, and sat her bottom down on top of the tissues. She heard another person enter the restroom and open the door to the stall next to hers. Amie glanced down at a pair of black Adidas running shoes on the floor next to her stall. She heard a thump, and Amie looked up over her right shoulder to the top of her stall partition. She screamed when she saw someone wearing a cap gazing down at her over the partition's ledge and recording a video of her. Amie pulled up her capris pants and then looked up at the top of the stall's partition. The video person was gone. Amie heard a collision at the door and a woman screaming, "Get out of here, pervert! Get out!"

Amie rushed out of the stall. "Did you see him? What did he look like?" she asked. She was breathing heavily and holding her hand over her heart. Her eyes were watery.

The screaming lady put her arm around Amie and said, "Calm down. No need to get hysterical. It's OK. I'm sure they'll catch him. Let me get security."

"The bastard might upload the video and share it on YouTube or Facebook," said Amie. Her hand shook as she dialed Patrick's number.

Screaming lady looked for help and reported the incident while Amie spoke to Patrick. Several minutes later, Amie met up with Cici in the card department, and Cici tried her best to comfort her. They couldn't leave Walmart until Amie explained the restroom events to security, the manager, and the police.

Needless to say, Amie postponed purchasing her patio furniture, and both of them exited the store. She spoke with Patrick at length about the incident again later that night.

"The lady who saw him leave the restroom gave a vague description of the man. He wore a cap, and she said he shielded his face when he collided with her. I feel so violated," she said. "From now on, I'm going to stay clear of public restrooms. What a warped person," Amie said.

Amie didn't even feel completely safe inside her own home after what had happened. She double-checked all the doors and sliders before going to bed, even though Patrick had told her he had locked up everything.

She sat down at her computer to search YouTube and Facebook to see if the bathroom incident was circulating. *Would that jerk post a video out there of me on the toilet?* She scrolled down. She drew in a deep breath and exhaled. She couldn't find any pictures or video of her sitting on her nest online.

When they were both in bed, Patrick asked her, "Are you OK?"

"It was an awful experience being filmed like that," Amie said. "I hope they find out who it is. I don't see how the police could, though, with the description given to them. Hundreds of men have dark hair, are about six feet tall, and wear jeans and sneakers," said Amie.

"I'm going to do a background check on Paul," said Patrick.

"What? Seriously? You think it was him?" asked Amie.

"Dark hair, six feet tall…He may have been the depraved paparazzo. I'll ask Crabbe to ask one of his former police buddies to activate a thorough background check on Paul—his education, employment, criminal record, credit history, motor vehicle and license record checks."

"I don't think Paul would do such a thing," Amie said. She turned out the bedroom light.

In the darkness of the room, Patrick said, "You never know, Amie. Good night, love."

During breakfast the next morning, there was a knock at their front door. "I'll get it." Patrick walked over to answer it. A delivery man was walking back to his white van. He had left behind a floral arrangement on the front step. Patrick brought the flowers inside and set them on the kitchen counter.

"For me?" asked Amie. "Did you send me these daisies and carnations?"

"No, it wasn't me," said Patrick. He picked up the attached note and read it to Amie. "Thank you for letting me know you'll show me houses. Sorry I got upset over you not calling me about the other house. Yours, Paul."

CHAPTER 2

Monday, May 18, while in her office at Cathell Realty, Amie checked her text messages. She saw one from Paul.

> *Call me. I want to house shop. Why are you ignoring me? Why aren't you doing your job?*

She dialed Patrick's cell phone. "Patrick, listen to this. It's irritating." She read the message Paul wrote to her.

Patrick said, "What a dick. Cut off communication with him. If you continue to answer his texts, it could just spur him on."

"So you want me to put a wall up?"

"Absolutely," said Patrick. "Don't get sucked in. Trust your instincts on this, Amie. Save and print out all the messages he sends to you. There will probably be more coming. I suggest you keep a log of his behavior. Record the date, time, and description of the incident each time. Again, don't respond to any of the messages he sends to you."

"I really have to do all that?" said Amie. "Now you're scaring me."

"He's stalking you, Amie. A real pattern seems to be developing. He's following you, showing up at your home and at the open house, leaving you messages, sending you flowers...what's next?" said Patrick. "If it continues, this could get serious."

"Oh dear God," said Amie. "You really think he's stalking me, and you think it's *that* serious?"

"Yes," said Paul. "I'm concerned this whole scenario could escalate. I met him when I was a detective back in Salisbury. He has a temper. He was extremely angry at me for not finding out who was responsible for breaking into his mother's house."

"Oh yeah, I remember that. I'm so fortunate I'm married to a PI. I really need your guidance and advice as to what to do right now. I wonder if psycho stalker knows that you own a private detective agency."

"I'm sure he does, and he doesn't care," said Patrick. "I'd like to crush him," Patrick said.

"No, Patrick, I don't want you to get into trouble because of him. I know you don't mean it. Listen, I have to get some shopping done at the Food Lion after work. I've got to go. I'll see you tonight," said Amie. She hung up.

This whole situation with Paul has me spooked. Wonder if I should contact the police now and file a report. I'd better listen to Patrick. He knows best in these situations. Don't want to talk to Paul and have it intensify things.

Amie's cell phoned pinged again. *Are you kidding me?* She looked at another message from Paul.

There's another house I want to see. Answer me.
What's your problem? Why didn't you call me
and thank me for the flowers?

Amie parked her Saab near the entrance to the Food Lion in the late afternoon. She grabbed a cart parked outside the automatic doors and headed inside. She picked up some avocados on the way to the soup aisle. She was placing two cans of cream of mushroom soup into her cart when Paul came out of nowhere. He grabbed Amie's arm. Her eyes enlarged at his sudden movement.

"Amie, why can't you meet with me? I have plenty of money to buy a house. The price doesn't matter. I have the money from my mother's house. Actually, I was well off even before I sold her house. If you find me a house on the water here, you would get a handsome commission. I'd be helping you out. You are so apathetic. Didn't another house just come up on Pintail on a canal, and I—"

"Let go of my arm!" said Amie. She wiped her clammy hands on her dress.

He removed his tinted sunglasses and squinted down at her, tightening his chiseled jaw.

Amie caught her breath and stared wide eyed at him. "I think it's best if you hire another realtor. My plate is pretty full right now, but I can recommend someone for you. He's really one of the best realtors in our office." She lifted her head and craned her neck to see if someone was coming down the soup aisle. But no one was in sight. Her stomach was in knots, and she felt her pulse beating in her ears. She held on to the shopping cart, wanting to slam it into his stomach. She imagined him taking a video of her inside the bathroom stall. Nausea filled her stomach.

"I want no one else to show me houses except you," said Paul. His eyes were smoldering as he glared at her.

"Please go away. Leave me alone, Paul." *Where is everybody? Doesn't somebody need soup?* Amie pushed her cart past him and hurried down the aisle toward the express checkout line in front of the store.

"Did you like the flowers?" he shouted after her.

She rolled her eyes and shook her head. Amie took a quick glance over her shoulder to see if Paul was behind her. He was nowhere to be seen. After paying for her few items, she became angry because she couldn't finish her food shopping because of him. She rushed out of the store, carrying her brown bag to her trusty Saab.

⚜

Paul relaxed on his small couch, with his legs protruding over one arm and his head resting on a square pillow on the other arm. He arched his eyebrows as he gazed at the photos of Amie and him, taken about seven years ago when they were a couple. *Man, she was hot—and still is.* Desire stirred in his blood. Seeing her briefly in her short floral-print sleeveless dress that day she caught him on her front lawn only increased his need for her. She had such a stunning figure that his mind just couldn't erase it. He decided to send her a quick email.

> *Amie, great seeing you at the Food Lion. Please call me. I'm anxious to move to Ocean Pines.*

Paul's May rent was overdue, and sitting at his desk, he filled out a check for the landlord. He wasn't sure how much longer he would live in this medium-sized, one-bedroom apartment. Even though Paul had inherited his mother's house in her will, he didn't want to live in such a huge house on the Wicomico River because it would be a lot of upkeep. Besides, that wasn't in his plans, and it was gloomy inside her house now that she no longer was alive.

He had adored his mother. She taught twelfth grade until she was sixty-four years old and was awarded "Best High School Math Teacher in Wicomico County." Paul's dad died when he was only eleven years old, and Paul's mother didn't have the heart to sell the house. So she and Paul lived there together for a long time. After her death, Paul sold the house for over $500,000 and added the cash to his already plentiful savings.

Especially now that his mom was gone, Paul longed to be with Amie again. He had never fully gotten over their breakup. He remembered how much his mother had cared for Amie. She had wanted Paul and Amie to live in the house that she could never give up. No matter what it took, he wanted Amie back with him.

He had despised Patrick. And still did. In 2010, a thief had broken into his mother's house. The intruder tied her up, taped her mouth shut, and got down to business—stealing anything of value in her home. When the thief was about to leave, he approached Paul's mother, who was tied to the dining room chair. He drew a knife and waved it in front of her face. She struggled with her bindings and screamed a muffled noise through the tape. Tears ran down her face. She struggled more, tilting the chair back and forth while the thief laughed at her. The chair toppled over on the hardwood floor. The burglar looked intently at her, then ignored her and walked into the kitchen. He popped opened a can of beer. After taking a few swigs, he left the can on the sink and carried the stolen goods to his car in his backpack.

Paul came home from work and was shocked at what he found. He helped his mother up from the floor, untied her hands, comforted her, and questioned her about the robbery. He called the police, and they arrived fifteen minutes later. His mother told the police that the burglar had worn a Michael Myers mask and never said a word. Sadly, his mother suffered a stroke a few days later.

Paul then met Patrick McCombe, who had been assigned the case when he was a detective in Salisbury. Patrick never captured the man who robbed Paul's mom and eventually caused her stroke. Paul's mother had never fully recovered from the stroke, and he had carried his bitterness toward Patrick with him, never forgetting Patrick's failure to capture the thief.

Paul's mother was extremely weak after the stroke. Her numbness and stiffness never disappeared, even after rehabilitation and time. Recognizing and remembering things were challenging for her. Paul stayed with his mother in her home, caring for her until the day she died.

He was so lonely and depressed without his mother. He felt trapped. He knew he had to move on but constantly fought against his loneliness. He had only a few friends. The loneliness was eating him alive day after day. He tried to hide his feelings from people at work and avoided talking about it to his coworkers, because he had felt they had their own problems to solve. So for the most part, he suppressed his sad feelings. Seeing other guys out with their girlfriends, laughing and having a good time, deepened his depression.

Paul's thoughts turned to Amie. He missed her enormously. He was desperate to be with her again. He had learned that she had married Patrick, but it wouldn't stop him from trying to see her. Paul knew he would have difficulty keeping tabs on Amie, because her schedule was so erratic. One day before seeing her in the Food Lion, Paul followed her in his company car to Berlin, then Fenwick Island, then west Ocean City, Selbyville, and Ocean Pines—all over the place, from Maryland to Delaware's eastern shores.

Boy, her job really keeps her hopping. If I resigned from my current job, there'd be more time to keep an eye on Amie's every step. I also could use the extra time to find a house in Ocean Pines. Don't think resigning from my job is wise, though. Could I really win Amie back? How could she have married a loser like Patrick? She didn't realize what I could give her. I have to make her see the light.

⚶

Amie doubted that Patrick was home yet and headed in her Saab to Discovery Investigations in Bishopville, Maryland, not too far from Ocean Pines. She called the office just to make sure he hadn't left. *Thank goodness, he's there.*

Amie walked into the waiting room outside Patrick's office. Amie opened the door to his office and stepped inside.

"Something's wrong. You look harried," said Patrick.

"Psycho stalker cornered me in the Food Lion, and he was pretty obnoxious. He frightened me."

Patrick asked Amie to sit down beside his desk and offered her a paper cup of water from the cooler. "You feel all right? Your face is crimson."

"I'm better now that I'm with you." She explained her entire encounter with Paul in the Food Lion.

"You need personal protection. Wait here. I'll be right back."

Amie glanced around his office and picked up the silver picture frame on his desk. She smiled. It was a photo of them on their honeymoon in Bermuda. After several minutes, Patrick came back with an assortment of items in his arms. He put them down on his desk.

"What's all this?" asked Amie.

Patrick said, "I'm going to protect my girl. One of these should do the trick if Paul makes you fear for your safety. Look at this device. It's a purple lipstick stun gun with three million volts and a flashlight."

"Geez," said Amie. "Is it easy to work?"

"I'll show you how to use each one. They're not difficult. Here's a mace pink lipstick pepper spray. It's easy to carry. Here's a whistle, and this is a pepper spray keychain. How about this baby? A multiguard stun gun."

Just then Joe Crabbe, his partner, walked into the office. "Hi, Amie. What's going on in here?" he asked.

Patrick said, "She's being stalked by her ex-boyfriend, Paul Simmons. Since you worked at the "OPPD" for nearly thirty years and have a great reputation there, do you mind getting one of your police buddies to do a complete background check on Simmons? I particularly need to know where he lives and what kind of car he drives, and I want his license plate numbers."

"I can do it myself. Not a problem," said Crabbe. He turned to Amie. "Looks like you're going to have to be careful, from what I see on Patrick's desk. A considerable number of stalkers once were in a romantic relationship with the person they were stalking. Regrettably, until he lands a hand on you, there's really nothing the police can do."

"Oh, that's just great, Joe," said Amie.

Patrick said, "Choose one, Amie."

"Really, Patrick?"

"Didn't you feel for your safety at the open house and at the Food Lion?" asked Patrick.

"Yes, of course I did," said Amie.

Pointing to his desk, Patrick said, "Which one do you want?"

"OK, well, I like the pink lipstick pepper thing," said Amie. "And I want the keychain too."

"Good choices," said Crabbe as he walked out of Patrick's office.

Amie said, "I'm not afraid to use these, but I'm scared to death of guns. I'm glad you didn't give me one. I wouldn't have taken it."

Patrick said, "OK. If you feel for your safety like you did before, don't hesitate to use your spray. Arm yourself in case he approaches you and frightens you again, especially at night after teaching Zumba classes at the community center."

"Patrick, you're freaking me out," said Amie.

"In the majority of stalking cases, there's not an explicit threat at first, but it can turn out to be threatening later. Joe's right. You have to watch out from now on," said Patrick. "Tonight, write down what happened today. Add it to your log. Don't forget the date and time."

"You already told me that. I won't forget. Do you think he was the one in the restroom stall?" asked Amie.

"Not any evidence. The cameras in Walmart weren't very helpful," said Patrick. "I want you to report what has been happening to you to the Ocean Pines Police Department."

"What can they do? You heard Joe," said Amie.

Patrick said, "I understand how you feel. They probably won't take it seriously. You need to start building your case, though, Amie. Most states treat stalking as a misdemeanor." Patrick reached for a book off his wall shelf. He flipped through the pages and said, "Look here. It says that stalking is the malicious course of conduct of approaching or pursuing a person with the intent to place a person in reasonable fear of bodily injury or death. At least you can file a report against him. You probably can apply for a court-ordered restraining order. We can contact a local prosecutor if need be. If you haven't told anyone about Paul stalking you, I'd recommend you share all of this with Cici, your other friends, and coworkers. They can also be on the lookout for you. I'd like to pummel him. I've had it with this creep."

"You've had it? I've had it!" said Amie. "I'm always looking over my shoulder to see if he's lurking there."

"I know, Amie. I feel helpless right now to help you. He has one hell of a nerve bothering you." Patrick gazed out the window.

Amie stared at Patrick as he looked out the window. *Hope he doesn't try to go after Paul.*

Amie left Patrick's office with her lipstick and keychain pepper spray. She decided to go to the police station the next day and report what was occurring. She'd follow Patrick's advice and tell everyone she knew.

The following morning, Thursday, May 21, Amie drove directly to the Ocean Pines Police Department and told them every detail. They were very understanding but couldn't put Paul in jail for what he had done. The police explained that his actions must continue over a period of time to be considered serious stalking. As Patrick had suggested, they did mention that maybe she could get a protective order if things worsened.

Amie headed to Cathell Realty for the rest of the day. She asked Bill Morgan, the top salesman, to take Paul on as a client and show him homes in Ocean Pines. She handed him Paul's business card.

Another realtor, Tina Logan, walked over. "Amie, after you told us about this Paul guy, I want to tell you what happened to one of my customers a few years ago. She broke up with her significant other, and a little time later, he showed up at her door with a Domino's pizza she hadn't ordered. As he stood there, holding the pizza, she slammed the door in his face. Later, her car was vandalized, and she looked out the window and saw him trespassing on her property. After that, he kept calling her and sending excessive messages to her email. She maintained a long laundry list for her case and saved everything he sent to her on her computer. Three months later, when her doorbell rang, she mistakenly opened her door, and he was standing there under the awning on her front porch. He told her he was carrying a gun and turned his back to her so she could see it. The gun was tucked beneath his belt, and she quickly shut the door, scared to death. That was the last straw for her, and she dialed 911. She eventually obtained a restraining order, and she didn't have more trouble after that."

"The magnitude of that is very scary," said Amie. "He'd better not show up at my front door with a gun in his belt. I just want this to be over."

Amie invited Joe and Cici to dinner at her house Friday evening. It was another pleasant, sunny day in May. Cici had some news for Amie and Patrick. They all sat on the outside deck, drinking their chilled white wine, except for Cici, and watched two Jet Skis motor in circles on the bay.

"So, what's this news you want to tell us?" asked Amie.

"I'm pregnant," said Cici. "And it's a miracle. Years ago, remember my gynecologist thought I probably couldn't have a baby because of my endometriosis?"

"Well, that wasn't accurate," said Amie. "That's such great news, Cici. She can call us Aunt Amie and Uncle Pat."

"She?" asked Joe. "He."

Cici said, "Joe wants a boy, and I wouldn't mind having a girl. But we want to be surprised."

"That would be so much fun, though, shopping for frilly, cute dresses," said Amie. "Can't wait. How far are you along? You're not even showing," said Amie.

"About two and a half months. I'm going to gain all my weight back and be fat again. I love being slender so much. It took me a while to achieve this thin body," said Cici. "I've kept the pounds off and haven't gained any weight in a whole year."

"Fat and pregnant works for me," said Joe, winking at Cici.

Cici said, "If it's a girl, when she's sixteen, I can't believe you'll be sixty-three years old."

Joe said, "That's the new forty-five." He bent his elbow and showed off his muscular arm.

Cici and Amie laughed. "I'll be in my fifties. We'll have to start saving for college now," said Cici.

Patrick said, "Hey, you guys, I have a great idea. If you're not busy, how about if we all spend Saturday night at the Hyatt Regency in Cambridge? It would be good for Amie to get away after what's been happening to her lately. What do you say?"

"It's a fantastic plan," said Cici. They all agreed that if the weather cooperated, they'd go.

Friday morning, sleeping through her iPhone alarm, Amie was late for work. She flew around the house, sipping her coffee, gathering a blank contract, dabbing her mouth with rose-colored lipstick, and brushing her hair. While she was fastening the clasp of her delicate necklace, the doorbell rang. She hurried over to open the door. And there was Paul.

Amie's lips parted, and she drew in a long breath. She began stuttering. "P-P-Paul, wha- what are you d-d-doing here?"

She looked around quickly. *Where's my lipstick spray?* Breathing uneasily, Amie felt a slight headache coming on.

"We need to talk," said Paul.

"I-I can't right now. I'm late for an appointment." She started to shut the door. Paul shoved his foot next to the bottom of the jamb before Amie could close the door.

"Let me in so we can discuss my house searching," he said with a sneer.

Is there a gun tucked in his belt? I need to take control. Amie glanced out to the street, and she spotted her neighbor walking her dog. She yelled out to her. "Mrs. Armstrong, how are you?"

Paul shifted to turn around to look. That brief moment was all it took for Amie to slam the front door on Paul, leaving Mrs. Armstrong no time to reply.

Amie leaned her body back on the closed front door and rested and waited. After seeing the time on her watch, she glanced out her living room window and saw that Paul was nowhere in sight. Still shaky, she gathered her things and left the house. She grabbed her lipstick pepper spray and held on to it tightly.

⊣⊢

Cambridge, Maryland, was only an hour from Ocean Pines. Amie, Patrick, Cici, and Joe all rode east on Route 50 in the same car. They pulled into the beautifully landscaped entranceway to their retreat.

"Look at that," Cici said. She pointed to a bald eagle atop a tall tree trunk without any branches or leaves.

"It's not real, Cici."

"It sure looks real," she said as Patrick sped by.

They chose valet parking rather than park a distance away from the hotel. After checking in, Amie unpacked, put her lipstick pepper spray in the drawer, and changed into her bathing suit, and then she and Patrick met Cici and Joe outside at the heated infinity pool. They claimed four lounge chairs. The pool overlooked the banks of the Choptank River.

"Time to get pampered," said Patrick. He ordered a grapefruit crush from the poolside waiter. Everyone else selected from the cocktail menu.

After swimming and soaking up the sun, Amie and Cici went to the Sago Spa and Salon. "I'm rejuvenated," said Amie. "So relaxing." They left the spa and found the guys in the hot tub. "When do you think you want to go to dinner?" asked Amie.

"I made reservations for 8:00 p.m. at the Water's Edge Grill," said Joe. "Prime rib for me," he said.

That evening, after a carefully prepared dinner at the restaurant, they decided to take a walk on the Hyatt's pier out on the Choptank River. The wind was blowing across the choppy water, and a family of ducks was near the river's edge. The riverbank was lined with buttercups.

"You had a rough day yesterday with your surprise visitor," said Patrick. "I hope you feel a little better now."

"This little getaway has helped, Patrick. It was a great idea. I love you and appreciate your suggesting this."

They missed the colorful sunset, but the sky was a lovely pink. Amie and Patrick continued walking around the resort, and Cici and Joe strolled over to the outside S'mores Hearth Fireplace. They sat down on the comfortable sofa and took it easy.

Early the next morning, they played mini golf, and Patrick didn't want to leave until he slid down the waterslide once more. They extended their checkout time to 1:00 p.m. "Hard to leave," said Amie. "Everything was so special. I'm revitalized," she said. Patrick squeezed her hand and kissed her forehead. "Thanks, Patrick. I had a wonderful time." He smiled back at her. Amie cupped her hand around his cheeks. Patrick hadn't shaved over the weekend. "I love your few days' growth of beard," Amie said. "I like the feel of it on my face. You are the sexiest animal."

"Animal?" said Patrick.

"OK. If you want to know, you're a very desirable man," said Amie.

"That's better," he said as he held her tightly and kissed her. He kissed her again. "Hmm, I think I'll keep my five o'clock shadow."

⊭

Entering their air-conditioned home in Ocean Pines after their weekend getaway was such a relief from the exceptionally warm weather. Patrick started putting things away while Amie also unpacked. "Have you seen my pepper spray keychain, Patrick? I didn't take it with me. I just took the lipstick one. I thought I left it here on top of my nightstand."

"No, I didn't touch it."

The bureau drawer that housed her underwear was open. Amie said, "My new lace bikini panties and red Victoria Secret push-up bra aren't here in my drawer."

"Probably in the hamper," said Patrick. He walked out of the bedroom. What he saw next was bizarre. In the kitchen, one place setting of Amie's favorite china and silverware, one ironed white cloth napkin, and one crystal glass of poured red wine garnished the glass-top round table. He stood there for what seemed an eternity, but it was actually only a minute. His stomach turned uneasily, and the hairs on back of his neck stood up. He went into the bedroom and retrieved his gun from the master bedroom closet.

"What are you doing?" asked Amie.

"Get into the bathroom and lock the door," he said.

Amie scurried to the bathroom.

Patrick searched everywhere possible inside the house. No one was there, but he had an idea who the intruder was. He went back into the bedroom and told Amie to come out of the bathroom.

"What in the world is wrong? Why do you have your gun?"

"Someone came inside our house while we were gone," Patrick said. "I combed the entire house. No one is here. Don't worry. I'm calling 911 and Crabbe. We need to get some fingerprints from the bedroom and kitchen."

"Do you think it was Paul?" asked Amie.

"Yep, but I have to prove it first. That son of a bitch."

"How in the world did he get in?"

"He's not so crafty. He broke the window in the guest bedroom. He probably used a hammer to break it. I'm changing all the locks," Patrick said. "I'm also going to install a camera outside in front of the house tomorrow."

After the detectives arrived, they dusted for prints but came up empty. None were found—not any on the merlot wine bottle, utensils, dish, glass, or bureau. Amie said, "Of course he must have worn gloves." Amie and Patrick were very disappointed, but they filed a police report.

Crabbe said, "Looks like your stalker could have paid you a visit."

"No doubt in my mind," said Patrick.

With strong resolve, both Patrick and Amie continued with their normal routine the next day. Time passed, and things were quiet for a while. Every day, Amie checked and rechecked her emails and text messages. Was Paul finally tired of harassing her? The good news was that three weeks had zipped by without a peep from the psycho stalker.

CHAPTER 3

The next morning at 7:00 a.m., Patrick and Crabbe unloaded the Walmart patio furniture and set the lounge chairs and tables around the pool area. "This should surprise Amie," said Patrick. He thanked Joe Crabbe for helping him to set up the furniture. Crabbe also had given Patrick the complete background check on Paul. "I appreciate it, Joe."

Crabbe said, "He works for Implant Products, Inc. in Salisbury, Maryland, and drives a silver Dodge Durango." He gave Patrick Paul's license number and address also. It was only a thirty-minute drive from Ocean Pines.

Patrick found out that Paul Simmons lived in a one-bedroom apartment near where Amie had gone to college. Paul paid his rent month to month on time. His company, Implant Products, developed products for elderly spine patients, ages sixty-five years and older, who had disorders such as osteoporosis and scoliosis. Also, the company provided implants for orthopedics, neurosurgery, and spinal surgery, as well as products for cardiology. Simmons sold the medical aids to hospitals and clinics, so he had a pretty decent job. He had graduated from Salisbury University with a degree in business. Paul Simmons had no criminal record, and he had incurred no debt. The information also included that Paul's mother's house had been sold recently.

"Joe, you did an in-depth job searching records from the Department of Motor Vehicles." Those records, among other information, yielded Paul Simmons's driving record. He had two speeding tickets, and a digital copy of his license photo was also included.

Just then, Patrick's cell phone vibrated in his pocket. He put the phone to his ear. "Mr. McCombe, this is Cindy Ross. I really need your help. I was in the dining room near our outside patio and overheard my husband, Jake, talking so amorously to this woman on his phone outside. He told her to meet him at the Bayfront Hotel on Sixty-Fifth in Ocean City. He said he would be there at check-in time at 3:00 p.m. It would be perfect if you could catch them and take pictures or a video of them together. I hope you're available to help me. Are you able to do that today? Or can one of your assistants do it?"

Patrick checked his watch and said, "Yes, I can do that. Actually, this is great news. Now I won't have to follow him around anymore if I can prove what you suspect. Saves time and money for you."

Mrs. Ross said, "And now I hope your surveillance will show Jake that I have proof that he *is* seeing another woman, and he can stop lying to me that he's not having an affair."

Patrick asked, "Mrs. Ross, have you found a number of prescription drug bottles in your home that neither you nor Mr. Ross is taking?"

"No, why?"

"I'll fill you in on it later. I have a few things to settle in Salisbury before I head to Ocean City, so I've got to hit the road," said Patrick.

Patrick gunned his engine veering onto Route 50 heading toward Salisbury. As he got closer to Salisbury, he was a three-minute cruise to Paul's apartment building, Shady Pines. He pulled his Cadillac Seville into the parking lot behind the building. His watch showed 8:05 a.m. He spotted Paul's silver Dodge Durango parked at the end of a row of cars. Keeping close tabs on the time, he sat and waited for Paul to come outside. He wished he could search his apartment to find Amie's stolen underwear, but he didn't have proof to do so.

Almost a half an hour later, Patrick saw Paul come out of his apartment building, and before he could reach his car, Patrick jogged over to him.

Paul raised his eyebrows, and his eyes expanded as he saw Patrick running toward him.

As he neared Paul, a little out of breath, Patrick said, "Back away from your car. We need to talk."

"What the hell do you want?" asked Paul.

"I want you to leave my wife alone. Simple as that," said Patrick.

"She's going to show me houses on the market in Ocean Pines. What's wrong with that? What, are you jealous?"

Patrick waved his finger in front of Paul's face. Rage gripped him. "You asshole. She doesn't want to show you anything. Keep away from her."

Paul laughed. "I'm not bothering her. I need to buy a house, that's all. I've got to go to work. Get out of my way."

"Let me search your apartment, you prick. I know you stole some things out of her bureau drawer."

Paul sneered and said, "You're crazy, man. Get the hell out of here. You're harassing me."

Patrick's anger spiked. Fury welled up in his chest and nearly consumed him. He grabbed Paul by his shirt collar. "If I ever hear that you bothered my wife again, you'll regret it."

"Let go of my shirt. Are you threatening me? I can report you to the police, scumbag," said Paul.

"Go right ahead, dickhead. Let's see who they believe." With a racing heart, Patrick walked back to his Seville. He pulled out onto Route 50, his foot pressing down hard on the accelerator. Glancing in his rearview mirror, he said, "I'm almost mad enough to kill him."

At 2:45 p. m. Patrick turned left onto Coastal Highway. He made a U-turn and drove into the front parking lot of the Bayfront Hotel and located a space for his car that would be perfect for observing when Cindy Ross's husband and his girlfriend arrived. At 3:05 p.m., he saw Ross's white Chevrolet Cobalt pull into the entrance to the lot. He recognized Jake Ross walking up the steps in front of the hotel carrying a huge black bag. Jake sat down on a concrete bench outside the hotel lobby doors and lit a cigarette.

Jake Ross was not a handsome man. He had dark, thick eyebrows; frizzy, inky-black hair; and a ruddy complexion. With his large, compact build, he'd be a tough match for Patrick. Periodically, his steely eyes scanned the parking lot. Ten minutes later, Jake saw his petite girlfriend and snubbed out his cigarette. She quickened her stride and skipped up the steps. Jake smacked her on the backside, and Patrick observed them embracing and kissing each other several times before entering the lobby doors. Patrick finished taking videos of them on his phone and called Crabbe.

"Joe, I may need you. I'm outside the Bayfront Hotel." He told Crabbe what he was up to.

Patrick walked into the lobby and took a video of them checking in and taking the elevator up to the second floor. He introduced himself to the staff at the reception desk and showed them his credentials. He walked back into the lobby and remained on the sofa, contemplating his next move.

He didn't have to think about it too long.

Female screams were heard inside Jake Ross's room. From a call inside the hotel, the police were contacted about an alleged domestic assault. When the police arrived, they went to the second floor in the elevator. Patrick followed a detective and one hotel staff person up the stairs. He trailed them past rooms 208 and 209 until they stopped at room 210, where people had reportedly heard objects being broken and the screaming of profanities at an ever-increasing volume.

Fortunately, Crabbe ran into the lobby after seeing patrol cars in front of the hotel and followed a detective to the second floor. He nodded to Patrick, who was near the door to Jake's room. Police knocked on the door and announced their presence. Inside, they heard a woman wailing and a man snarling loudly. They tried to open the door, but Jake had barricaded it shut with a bureau. It took tons of effort for the men to kick in the door.

Once the police, Patrick, and Crabbe gained entry, they found the room in disarray, with two shattered lamps, a broken nightstand, and a woman's G-string and strapless bra on the floor. On a round table in the room were assorted bottles of prescription drugs—more than three hundred prescription pills—oxycodone, hydrocodone, Percocet, Ritalin, Valium, and Vicodin. A regular little pharmacy. On top of the small refrigerator was Jake's Smith and Wesson.

With her hands covering her face, the petite woman, dressed in a robe, was sitting on the bed sobbing. She pointed to the balcony when asked about Jake's whereabouts. She composed herself and then said that Jake had fled toward the balcony after the police broke through the door.

Patrick went out to the balcony, looked over the railing, and saw Jake swimming in Assawoman Bay, directly below the second-story deck. Crabbe and Patrick rushed out of the room, raced down the stairwell, and entered the bay waters. After swimming stroke after stroke and kicking their legs wildly, they retrieved him from the water. Patrick held on to Jake's tank top. Both of them were out of breath when they tugged Jake up a ramp toward the hotel and snapped the handcuffs around his wrists. Good thing Crabbe had come along because it took the two of them to pull Jake ashore.

Patrick was glad the police had been involved in the case. They searched Jake's Chevrolet and found a large amount of drugs and mushrooms. As far as Cindy Ross was concerned, she had the ammunition she needed to obtain her divorce. Patrick told her he would hook her up with the attorney in Salisbury who had helped Cici obtain a divorce from her ex-husband.

Case closed. Patrick grinned and shook Crabbe's hand. When they left the hotel, he and Crabbe went to the Purple Moose to celebrate, even though they were soaking wet. Patrick thanked Crabbe profusely. "Without you, that dude would have broken my back trying to get him out of the water," Patrick said.

Crabbed laughed. "He was a mighty bulky, barrel-chested guy," said Crabbe. "My back's killing me right now." They both laughed and clinked their Blue Moon beer bottles.

Later, Patrick learned that Jake had burglarized numerous houses in the Delmarva area, stealing prescription drugs from homeowners' medicine cabinets. Jake was charged with possession of controlled dangerous substances with the intent to distribute. He also was charged with gun possession. He was seen by a Maryland district court commissioner and transferred to the Worcester County Jail, where he was being held without bail.

CHAPTER 4

Molten anger had rolled through Paul's veins after his encounter with Patrick in his parking lot. *Bastard. No good freakin' detective.* He seethed inside on his way to work and put off his plan for the day to go to Ocean Pines during his lunch hour. He would have to wait. He swallowed down his frustration and was determined to stick it to Amie for rebuking him in the Food Lion. That night, he sat in front of his computer for a long time, and then he started pounding away on the keys.

TO: opcathellrealty.com

SUBJECT: Amie McCombe

Amie McCombe is an incompetent employee of Cathell Realty. Amie McCombe refused to help me find a house in Ocean Pines. She sold a house on a canal that I wanted to a couple right from under my nose after I told her I was interested in buying it. She's irresponsible. She refused to help me further to find a house even though I told her that price was no object. She has a sexual history that is disgraceful. Amie McCombe has solicited for sexual relationships with at least a hundred men. She makes more money as a prostitute than she does in real estate sales. She stoops to the lowest level possible as a woman to do whatever men ask for sexually. Amie McCombe is a reprehensible and discreditable human being.

He smirked as he read his comments. *Just wait, Amie…would love to see your face when you see this email I sent to your brokerage.* Remembering Russell Crowe's words in the movie *Beautiful Mind*, Paul said aloud, "She'll be mortified, terrified, petrified, and stupefied by me."

He then decided to send his comments to every realtor who worked there. Paul looked up their individual email addresses online. *Wish I could be a fly on the wall at Cathell Realty tomorrow.* He made sure the realtor extraordinaire, Bill Morgan, especially got the email.

Don't need him to find me a house.

Paul laughed out loud. He felt resuscitated.

That night, Paul snuggled in bed with Amie's silky bra and bikini panties next to his cheek.

⚹

Amie was relieved that Patrick's drug case was solved and that he was out of danger. She dressed in a long-sleeve fuchsia dress for work. It was a cool, overcast day for June. She had to attend a meeting in the realtors' office. When she walked into the conference room, all her coworkers were seated around the long mahogany table. Mr. Cathell was at the head of the table. All eyes were on Amie.

"Something's up," said Amie. "Why are you all looking at me that way?"

Mr. Cathell said, "Amie, your stalker is back. He has sent an email to each of us. We saved all of them. But don't worry; we have your back. I called my friend, Chief of Police Hank Phillips, and he's coming over."

"You must mean Hulk," said Amie. "The largest man you've ever seen." Amie knew him from Cici's husband's trial a year ago. Cici's husband, Greg, had attacked Cici in their bathroom and knocked her unconscious, causing a concussion. Hulk, Patrick, and Crabbe knew one another well, working on that case as well as other intriguing cases in the past.

The group showed Amie the email from Paul. She silently read his email.

"Writing explicit false information about my sex life…You know it's all untrue," she said as she looked around the conference table.

"Yes, Amie, of course we do," said the group.

Amie's eyes welled up. "I can't believe he would stoop to this. My husband told me this whole situation could escalate."

When Hulk arrived, Amie explained to him what she had experienced the last two months with Paul Simmons. She thought Hulk had put on a few more pounds on his 350-pound frame since she last saw him.

"He's angry as hell," said Hulk as he read the email. "Amie, I'll explain some safety strategies for you to incorporate after incidents like this with him." He went into great detail about how to protect herself. Amie took note of one strategy he mentioned.

"When inside a restaurant, sit with your back to the wall, and watch the entrance," he said. It was good advice for all the group to hear. And Amie filed another police report before she went home.

⚎

When Patrick entered the back kitchen door and didn't see Amie in the kitchen, he called out her name. He walked into their bedroom and found her face down on their bed crying. "What's wrong, hon?"

Amie told him about the nasty emails that Paul had sent.

"Your coworkers don't believe such nonsense and know the real you. Sweetheart, don't get upset thinking they believe that."

Amie said, "The emails he sent to them will still make me feel uncomfortable being around them every day. I hope they believe it's all fabricated. That sex stuff he made up was so humiliating." Tears blurred her eyes.

"Amie, stop worrying about them. If they only knew how much you turn me on, you sexy thing," said Patrick. He grabbed her and kissed her again and again.

"Stop," Amie said, and then she started giggling. "Stop, Patrick. Stop. I have to get ready for my Zumba class." She laughed when she saw Patrick's bottom lip curl down as she left.

It was a drenching downpour that night when Amie left the Ocean Pines Community Center after teaching her dance class. She had an unsettled feeling that she was being watched as she headed toward her car. *Should not have lingered and should have walked out with Cici. Stupid.*

Amie didn't have an umbrella and got completely soaked. She fumbled in her purse for her lipstick spray and dashed to her Saab. The car wouldn't start at first, but then it kicked in. She drove a few more blocks; then the Saab died on her. She drifted to the side of Ocean Parkway without descending into the gulley. She called Patrick, and he said he was on his way and would be there in a few minutes to pick her up. Amie sat there in the darkness. Her body twitched as she heard a thump at the rear of her car. Her heart pounded faster, and her chest was moving up and down under her two layers of clothing.

Amie took several deep breaths to calm herself. With a trembling hand, she wiped her brow. *Hurry, Patrick.* The rain poured down on the roof of her car, and the water pelted the windshield.

Clunk. Smack. "Aaaaah!" she yelled. Her rain-drenched body was shivering. She saw a black shadow race past the other side of her car. *Trust your instincts, girl.* She immediately pounded on the horn. *Its blaring sound should scare him away.* Patrick's headlights were heading toward her Saab. He swerved over in front of her stalled car and got out of his Seville.

Amie wound down her window. "Are you OK?" said Patrick.

"He was here, outside my car. I just know it," Amie said. She got out of the Saab.

"Well, no one is around here now. You're safe," he said. He hugged Amie tightly and walked her to his car.

When they arrived home, after Amie dressed in dry clothes, she and Patrick had a short discussion in the living room.

"You said to ignore Paul and don't communicate with him because things could escalate. I listened to you. So why do you think he sent those horrible emails to my coworkers? And you know it could have been him by my car tonight. It scared the pants off me," Amie said.

"I think it's my fault, Amie," said Patrick.

"Why?"

"Because I confronted him at his apartment," said Patrick.

"You did what? Why in heavens would you do that?"

"It was foolish, I know. I was so pissed off at him for what he's doing to you. I thought it could be over when you didn't hear from him anymore." Patrick explained the altercation he had had with Paul in the parking lot.

Amie said, "Thanks a lot."

"I know," said Patrick. "I'm sorry, Amie. I want you to file for a restraining order."

"I'll file for one first thing in the morning," said Amie.

That night they fell asleep to the sounds of thunder and hammering rain on the roof of their house.

⚜

At 7:15 a.m. the next morning, Patrick watched his mug fill from his Keurig coffee maker and glanced out the wide glass kitchen window. "Amie, come here! In the kitchen!"

She hustled in, in her robe, over to where Patrick was pointing out their huge window. Her mouth dropped open. Bobbing cushions and pillows covered the top of the water in their pool, and all their newly purchased outdoor furniture from Walmart lay at the bottom of it.

"The storm couldn't have done all that," said Patrick. "That idiot is messing with us again."

"I'm calling Cici's lawyer to get that restraining order. He's the best," said Amie.

That same day, June 19, Amie called Ted Berry, a local, very successful prosecutor in Worcester County. Amie knew Mr. Berry, also known as "Bear," from when Cici's husband was on trial for the abduction and assault on her two years ago. He successfully put Cici's monster of a husband in jail.

Mr. Berry's office was located in Berlin, Maryland. She didn't speak to him personally, but his receptionist set up an appointment for Amie at 4:45 that afternoon.

Inside his plain, untidy office, Amie shook his hand and admired his good looks. She told Mr. Berry that Paul Simmons's unwanted contact was making her feel threatened. She told him that she feared he would cause her bodily injury, even though he hadn't assaulted her. Amie explained everything that had happened since that day Paul was on her front lawn. She also showed him her log.

Berry said, "He hasn't physically harmed you, but I certainly can see why you would be frightened for your safety after what he has done so far. He seems to be upping the ante with the last email he sent. I don't want to alarm you, but he could eventually end up injuring you. Unfortunately, to be eligible for a protective or restraining order, you must fall into a certain category. For example, you have to have had a sexual relationship with him within one year before filing for relief, or you have to be related to him by blood or marriage. There are seven categories to qualify for a restraining order, and none of them apply in your situation. You told me that you hadn't seen him for at least five years before he came to your house. Since you don't qualify for a protective order, you may be able to file for a peace order. I advise you to still save all your police reports and continue your documentation."

Amie asked, "What is a peace order?"

Berry said, "A peace order is a form of legal protection for anyone who is experiencing problems with an individual. It enables a person who wishes to be left alone to ask the court to order another person—in this case, Paul Simmons—to stay away and refrain from any contact with you. Peace orders cover acts such as harassment, stalking, and trespassing."

"When can I file for this?" asked Amie.

"There are a few steps. You have thirty days after the act occurs to file a petition with the court," Berry said. "You also have to take an oath when filing for an interim peace order. There is a penalty for providing false information, which I'm sure you're not doing. The filing fee is around fifty dollars, and there's a forty-dollar service fee."

Amie said, "I have to pay to keep him away from me? That's a real bummer."

"Yes," said Berry. "But believe it or not, there are people out there who lie about individuals threatening them and causing them harm."

"Tell me what to do from here," said Amie.

"You can seek relief without a lawyer. Get copies of your police reports. Get someone to testify on your behalf. You have to fill out a petition at the office of the district court commissioner. After submitting the petition, you will have to appear before a commissioner to explain your reason for seeking relief. You hold the burden of proof by reasonable grounds to establish that an incident occurred between you and Paul Simmons. In your case, you have proof of harassment from your police reports and witnesses."

Amie said, "This is all so detailed and complicated. What kinds of things would be on my peace order to protect me from Simmons?"

"Well, the district court commissioner may order that Simmons refrain from contacting or harassing you; or order him to refrain from entering your house and remain away from your job; or refrain from committing an act against you," said Berry. "After you file an interim peace order, you will appear before a judge to explain your reason for seeking relief. Again you will have to present the burden of proof. The judge can order to refrain Simmons for the same things as the commissioner ordered. You must attend a final peace order hearing for obtaining long-term protection. Both you and Simmons will attend a formal hearing. Simmons will be cross-examined and will have an opportunity to disprove your case. Do not be surprised if he lies about what happened. At the conclusion of the hearing, the judge will decide whether an act occurred and whether it is likely that Simmons will commit a similar act in the future."

"Seriously?" asked Amie. "This is all too much. I feel like he's in complete control, and I can't put out the fires. It involves a lot of time and energy."

"Yes, it does. That's the law," said Berry.

Amie left his office, her head hanging down. *Feels like I can't win. It's a lost cause.*

CHAPTER 5

"There's too much involved, Patrick. I'm not going to file a petition for a peace order. It's ridiculous and takes a long time and several visits to court. I wouldn't feel comfortable not hiring a lawyer, and it would cost money to get Paul off my back. It's such a shame," Amie said. "You and Crabbe are right. The police don't take stalking seriously."

"I support you in your decision," said Patrick.

"But if it were you, you'd file a peace order, right?" asked Amie.

"I don't want to see you upset about this," said Patrick. "And don't worry about what I think. I just don't want him to bother you."

"I'm upset, but I'm not filing," said Amie. "Maybe I'll carry a lipstick stun gun instead of a lipstick spray."

"Amie, do whatever you like. Seriously, I want you to be especially careful, because I signed up to attend a conference again this year. It's that Maryland Association Training of Licensed Investigators and the Criminal Defense Investigation

Training Council Conference. They've joined forces to deliver what they promised would be the most exciting training event of the year. I don't want to miss it. It's only a forty-hour conference at the Criminal Defense Investigative Academy in Dover, Delaware. They're offering a variety of training courses that I'm going to need. Joe is going to attend also. Maybe you could skip teaching your Zumba class this week."

"It's fine. I know you enjoyed last year's conference," said Amie. "And it's not like you'll be gone for a week."

"I'll get you that stun gun and review with you how to use it," said Patrick.

"Thanks," Amie said. "Cici and I can stay together while you two are gone."

"I was just about to suggest that," said Patrick.

Patrick and Joe Crabbe left for their conference two days later. The night before, Amie checked her emails...and there it was. Paul had sent a repugnant message. She didn't tell Patrick, but she printed it out and saved it for her case's laundry list.

> Amie, all I wanted from you was to see you again, since I decided to move to Ocean Pines. I just thought you'd want to help me because we had a past together, and you once had feelings for me. I had hopes of marrying you. You treat me like I have the plague. You'll see one day that you can't treat people that way. You're a bona fide witch. As a person, you stink. You're immoral and cruel.

The day Paul and Crabbe left for the conference in Dover, Amie visited the police department in Ocean Pines again, showed them the email, and filed another report. Amie then headed to her office for a settlement on a house and showed two houses after that. Business was good. The day flew by, and before Cici came over to spend the night, Amie wanted to give her house a quick cleaning.

Dust had accumulated over the week, since Amie had left her windows open a few days for fresh air. It turned out to be a meticulous cleaning. Amie polished the furniture, washed the floors, and scoured the sinks and the master bathroom shower stall. After vacuuming the carpets in the living room and dining room, she headed to clean the powder room.

She stopped in her tracks. What she saw shocked her and made her sick to her stomach. There was a mass of poop all over the top of the toilet seat. A message was scrawled on the bathroom mirror above the sink written in bright-red lipstick.

> *If you prick us, do we not bleed? If you tickle us,*
> *do we not laugh? If you poison us, do we not die?*
> *And if you wrong us, shall we not revenge?*

She freaked out and ran into the bedroom to fetch her stun gun. She went into every room of the house, stun gun in hand.

Amie raised her voice. "Where are you, you bastard? Afraid to come out? I'm not scared of you, you sick puppy. You're perverse. I'm calling 911. Did you hear that? I'm calling the police." She also called Cici.

Detectives arrived fifteen minutes later. They told her not to touch anything in the bathroom. The smell was disgusting. They took DNA samples from the top of the toilet seat, snapped pictures of the message on the mirror, and spread fingerprint powder around the bathroom.

"Could you please clean up all the poop for me? I don't want to do it," Amie said.

They had come prepared. The cleaning squad, in white coveralls and rubber gloves, set to work. "Ugh. He smeared poop all over the top," said the cleaning cop. Disinfecting took a while. The smell of bleach permeated the house.

"Why would anyone do such a repulsive thing?" Amie asked one detective.

"We've seen this before," he said. "He's saying 'screw you.' But maybe not specifically you; maybe your husband. We caught a serial pooper who defecated in a washing machine when clothes were inside. We'll use the poop sample to track your guy. Did he take a dump anywhere else?"

Amie's face turned pale. "I don't think so," Amie said. "And he's not *my* guy. How did he get into my house? We have a camera installed out front and a motion detector light by the front door."

"One of our guys checked outside. The intruder entered through the sunroom's door, breaking the glass window pane above the doorknob. We dusted for prints."

The police allowed Cici to come in. She listened as Amie filed another report with the police. Amie thanked them after they dusted for fingerprints and sanitized the bathroom. She heard one of the detectives on his way out say, "That was a crappy job." She could hear their loud guffaws as they walked outside to their patrol cars.

Amie sprayed the house with superstrength air freshener. She reluctantly stepped into the powder room and inspected the toilet, looking for something the cop cleaners might have missed. *I want it spotless in here.* Feeling dirty after just being in the bathroom, Amie washed her hands three times in hot, soapy water and then doused them with hydrogen peroxide. She walked into the kitchen and opened the wine cooler, where she had saved a good bottle of Cabernet Sauvignon. "I need this," she said to Cici.

"I'll definitely join you, but instead, I'll have some ginger ale if you have it."

They sat down on the sofa sipping their drinks. Amie took several deep breaths. "Aaah, tastes great."

"Wish I could have some," Cici said.

"You'll have to wait until Thanksgiving. I'm glad you're here, Cici. That was despicable and nauseating. Wait until I tell Patrick."

"Poop man is nuts and needs to be committed. Here, drink some more wine," Cici said.

"Oh no," Amie said. "No. No, no." She ran out of the room.

"What's the matter? Where are you going?" asked Cici as she followed her with her arms held up in the air.

"The washing machine! I need to check it. He might have pooped in it!"

⚔

Patrick slammed his fist on the dining room table when he heard that their home had been broken into and excrement left on their toilet seat. "Fucking asshole. It had to be him again."

Amie said, "He sent me an email that I stink as a person. He literally stinks as a person. He's going to pay for this."

"Oh, you bet he is," said Patrick as he drew in his eyebrows and tightly closed his lips until they were narrow and thin. He shook his head. "You were lucky he wasn't here when you came home from work. He could have hurt you." Patrick paused. "He's been watching us. He must have known I was gone," Patrick said. "I don't like his message on the mirror. He either thinks he got his revenge by doing what he did, or he's planning on more retaliation."

Patrick called the Ocean Pines Police Department, identified himself, and asked if they had any more news regarding the break-in. Hulk Phillips told Patrick and Amie that after the incident in their bathroom, they had contacted Paul and asked him for a DNA sample. Surprisingly, he had obliged. Patrick was glad the police had retrieved a DNA sample from Paul. The police department had good reason, since Paul had recently sent those nasty emails, and they had reports of his harassment of Amie. Unfortunately, Hulk told Patrick that no fingerprints were found on the sunroom's glass window or in the bathroom. All areas seemed to be wiped clean.

"All we can do now is wait for the DNA results," said Patrick.

"Don't you think he's smart enough to know that his DNA will connect him to the poop?" asked Amie.

"Who knows? Maybe it wasn't his, or maybe it was horse manure."

"Patrick, really? Can you buy us a new toilet seat at Home Depot? And I don't want you to go after him again," Amie said. "Stay clear of him, please."

"Not planning to go after him, but I'd like to pulverize him. I'm curious to know what he's up to next. And yes, I'll get you a new toilet seat," said Patrick.

While Amie was at work the next day, Patrick called Crabbe. "Joe, can you put a tail on the Mad Pooper? I'd do it myself, but he might be following me as well as Amie."

"Absolutely. Can do," said Crabbe.

"Thanks, Joe."

"Can't believe he pooped on top of your toilet," said Crabbe.

Patrick said, "Yeah, he's a real mental case. That reminds me, I have to install a camera in the rear of the house. I'm going to get his ass."

On Tuesday, June 23, Joe Crabbe borrowed Cici's car to follow Paul. He wanted to alternate his vehicle with hers, just to make sure Paul wouldn't detect that he was tailing him. His first day, Crabbe followed Paul to Peninsula General Hospital in Salisbury and then to Subway after Paul's trip to a medical center. Paul then drove to his apartment, where he stayed the rest of the night. Day two, Paul proceeded first thing in the morning to the law office of defense attorney Jim Reynolds, on Coastal Highway in Ocean City. After spending a little over half an hour there, Crabbe followed Paul to Implant Products, Inc. back in Salisbury. The next morning, Paul headed to Ocean Pines, and Crabbe observed him looking at houses there. No realtor met him. He was apparently doing this on his own.

Paul stopped on a few occasions in front of houses for sale but remained in his car. He would then drive off to analyze his next choice. On occasion, Paul left his car to inspect houses that were farther back from the street and located on partially or heavily wooded lots. One was on a woody, quiet cul-de-sac. The houses that Paul surveyed were small in size, mainly A-frames or tiny ranchers nestled in the woods. Crabbe guessed that each was approximately 1,200 to 1,500 square feet. The homes were modest and inexpensive compared to other homes in Ocean Pines. The last one, Paul observed, looked neglected and was on Manklin Creek with a private backyard. Crabbe shook his head. *Thought he wanted a house on the water.*

After Paul had given all those houses the once-over by walking around each one, Crabbe followed him as he drove over the bridge that exited the Ocean Pines community. Crabbe pursued him on Route 113 as he turned into the parking lot of Atlantic General Hospital in Berlin. After Paul's appointment at the hospital, Crabbe observed him driving back to his Salisbury apartment. On Friday, Crabbe waited outside in his car as Paul spent time inside a local clinic. Then Paul spent the rest his day at Implant Products.

At the end of the workweek, Paul walked outside with a number of people, laughing and talking loudly. He headed to Roadie Joe's Bar and Grill around 5:15 p.m. Crabbe watched him park his Durango and walk over to the bar and join several peers. Crabbe surmised he was joining his coworkers for drinks and appetizers during happy hour. Inside the bar, Crabbe remained in the back where he could watch Paul but wouldn't be noticed. He heard his cell phone ping in the midst of all the bar commotion. He walked outside to read a text just sent to him.

It was from Patrick. *We have the DNA results back from the lab. It's Paul's poop.*

CHAPTER 6

Paul was still not over his unwavering anger toward Amie for snubbing him. *How dare she turn her back on me.* He knew the police would get a DNA sample off Amie's toilet seat. He willingly gave permission for Hulk to get a sample because it would look bad if he didn't oblige, and he felt Patrick would figure out a way to get a sample somehow anyway.

He drove to Ocean City to meet with his defense lawyer, Jim Reynolds, for a second time. On his way to his lawyer's office, he thought how much pleasure it had given him to defecate in their home. *Bet Patrick was fuming and lost it when he found out. He took Amie from me. He deserves what I did.*

The law offices were located in a one-story gray rectangular building directly on Coastal Highway. Six large-paned windows faced the street. Paul parked in the lot behind the building and walked around to the front. He climbed up five steps and entered the lobby. He found his attorney's office down the hall on the right. Paul announced his arrival in the small reception area and walked over to select a magazine from the wall mount. Before he grabbed his selection, the secretary said he could see Mr. Reynolds.

"Good morning, Mr. Simmons," said Reynolds. His lawyer had large, close-set eyes, olive-colored skin, and thick, untamed hair. They shook hands. "Have a seat."

"Thank you," said Paul. Piles of manila folders were on top of the left corner of Jim Reynolds's desk. Paul took a seat in a brown leather chair in front of the desk and scanned the twelve-by-twelve office. Three white bookcases lined the wall behind the desk. To the right of the desk, a large-paned window faced a busy side street.

Reynolds turned in his swivel chair. "Let's see now." He scratched his broad nose, looking down at papers inside a folder. "Um...last time, you wanted me to help you draw up your will, and you explained that you broke into this guy Patrick's home in Ocean Pines and left him a present on his commode, correct?"

"Yes," said Paul. "Guilty as charged. The cops took a DNA sample of my feces, and they will connect it to me. I hate this guy Patrick McCombe." He explained to his lawyer what he thought Patrick had failed to do when his mother was robbed. "I've always harbored revenge."

"No one was home when you broke into the house, right?" asked Reynolds.

"That's right," said Paul. "Both of them were at work."

"What makes you so sure?" asked Reynolds.

"I called both of their offices to see if they were there," said Paul.

"You know, that's a pretty disgusting thing to do," said Reynolds.

"I know. Like I said, I wanted revenge." said Paul. "I didn't plan to do what I actually did in the bathroom. I wanted to vandalize or deface his house in some way, but it ended up that I did what I did instead."

His lawyer arched his unruly eyebrows. "Don't you have any remorse?"

Paul just shrugged a couple of times. *What I did was more for Patrick, not Amie.*

"So you say the DNA results will prove it was you. Well, since that's the case, you will undoubtedly be charged with criminal mischief," said Reynolds. "It's a misdemeanor."

"Can the criminal mischief charge be dropped?" asked Paul.

"It's not predictable."

"What is the penalty for it?" asked Paul.

"It depends on a number of things, like if you've committed other offenses. Usually you have to pay a fine," said Reynolds.

Paul smiled and shook his head. "That's what I thought. I hope that you can get me off easy," said Paul. "You come highly recommended." Their discussion lasted about twenty minutes more.

"I'll be in touch and let you know when we'll have to go to court," said his lawyer.

Paul did not mention Amie at all, but he hoped he'd see her in court. He walked out of his lawyer's office, down the hall, and back out to the lobby. *Reynolds looked at me like I was some kind of nut.*

Court was held on a humid day in July. Paul wiped the sweat from his brow and sat in the pew smartly dressed in his black suit and silk tie.

The district courthouse was in Snow Hill, Maryland, near the Pocomoke River where bald cypress trees line its banks. Snow Hill, the county seat of Worcester County, Maryland, has a population of 2,100 people and was established in 1686 by English settlers. Major fires in 1844 and 1893 destroyed the center of Snow Hill, including two successive courthouses.

Patrick was looking forward to the court's proceedings. He sat near the front of the courtroom so he could hear Jim Reynold's arguments. Amie decided not to go. Judge Michael Wiseman was presiding. He was a portly man with not a hair on his head.

Paul searched the pews for Amie. He spotted Patrick. *Where is she?*

He snapped to attention when Judge Wiseman addressed him and his lawyer. Wiseman's chin jutted out from his square jaw when he spoke. His voice sounded hoarse, as if he had a sore throat.

Judge Wiseman said to Paul and his lawyer, "Mr. Simmons, you have been charged with criminal mischief. This is a crime which involves any damage, defacing, alteration, or destruction of tangible property with criminal intent." The judge cleared his throat. "Mr. Reynolds, how does your client plead?"

Jim Reynolds turned to Paul. Paul admitted he was guilty of the misdemeanor of criminal mischief. Paul gave the judge a brief description of what he had done and what his original intent was.

"I'm so sorry for what I did, Your Honor," said Paul. "I am guilty of breaking into Mr. McCombe's home and defacing his property. I can't stand the guy and wanted to get even with him for something he did to my family." Paul scanned the room again. No sign of Amie.

"Your Honor, my client did have criminal intent to deface Mr. McCombe's property. What he chose to do was a vulgar act, no question. Mr. Simmons is a first-time offender and has never done anything like this before. I ask the court that Mr. Simmons receive the minimum penalty for this misdemeanor."

Judge Wiseman said, "Your client broke a glass window in order to enter Mr. McCombe's home. Mr. Simmons, you admitted you entered the property and had the intent to damage, destroy, or deface the McCombe's home. Shame on you, Mr. Simmons. The act you committed was repulsive. I don't care how much you hated the guy," Judge Wiseman said. "I won't recommend you serve any jail time for this; however, committing criminal mischief is generally tied to the value of the damage that has been done, including whether you have done it previously and have been charged or convicted of a crime of any type. First-time offenders are often sentenced to pay a fine. But in your case, I want to place you on a sentence of probation for one year in addition to sentencing you with a fine. Mr. Simmons, you are sentenced to pay a fine of $1,500 to the court and $300 to cover the cost for the broken glass window for restitution. When the court orders you to serve probation, you must meet specific terms. For example, in this case, you cannot commit any more crimes; you must meet regularly with the probation officer; you may not associate with any other criminal; you must pay all fines and restitution; you must maintain employment; and you must stay away from the victims in the house you defaced, and that includes no contact of any kind with them. Next case, please," said the judge.

Paul was pleased that the hearing had been a speedy one but not pleased about the probation part. He was also disappointed he didn't see Amie. He turned to his lawyer. "I can't believe I've been put on probation," said Paul. "Can't you drop that part of my sentencing?"

Reynolds said, "Paul, you're lucky the judge didn't have you serve time in jail. Sorry, no, I can't drop the probation sentence." Under his breath, with his back turned a few feet away from Paul, he said, "Don't care for this guy at all. If he poops on top of my toilet, I'll kill him."

CHAPTER 7

"Great news about Paul," said Amie. "Serves him right."

"It's a slap on the hand in my opinion," said Patrick. "Amie, if he had the nerve to break into our house, send you messages, follow you around, and do what he did, I don't really trust that he's going to stay away from you. This guy's got balls, and he's clearly out of his mind."

Amie said, "I agree. He's deranged. He wanted to get back at you, right? That's what you told me he said in court. And the subject of him stalking me wasn't the issue in this case."

"No, they concentrated on what he actually did in our house. He most likely has a vendetta against both of us, and that's why I just don't feel he's completely satisfied that he has fully gotten his revenge."

"Do you know who his probation officer is?" asked Amie.

"Yes, I have his name. I'll keep tabs on Paul honoring his appointments with him. Listen, Amie, this has been traumatic for both of us. It's a gorgeous day. Let's take the pontoon out tonight and have dinner on the Saint Martin's River while watching the sunset. Just the two of us."

"That would be nice," said Amie. "And thanks for installing the new toilet seat this morning."

Later that evening, Amie and Patrick's arms were full carrying items for their dinner as they walked to the pier, passing their fifteen-by-twenty-foot in-ground pool in the center of their backyard. It was the right night for watching a sunset. Amie walked down to the edge of their pier carrying paper plates and utensils while Patrick removed the canvas from the seats and raised the black canopy on their pontoon and snapped it into place. He stepped back onto the pier and stood next to Amie. They viewed the loveliness of the evening overlooking Assawoman Bay standing at the end of their wooden wharf. Patrick loaded the basket with their dinner onto the boat and helped Amie step inside it. He took the helm, and they cruised under the Ocean City Route 90 Bridge and headed toward Saint Martin's River. He let the pontoon drift without lowering the anchor into the sizable waterway. It was odd, but not many boats ever cruised the river after 7:00 p.m. in the summer months. In fact, except for two Jet Skis and one boat pulling a water skier, no other boats were in sight. Patrick and Amie thought boat owners were missing so much by not experiencing an impressive sunset in the evening on the water.

Their dinner menu consisted of chicken salad, pasta, cucumber and tomato salad, corn bread, and a chilled bottle of sauvignon blanc. The skies were tinted pink and red. The cirrus clouds did not interfere with blocking the magnificent, glowing sun. The sunlight shimmered in the water, spotlighting the numerous jellyfish. Dinner was more appetizing at the pontoon restaurant because of the picturesque scenery. Patrick stretched out on the pontoon's cushions, and Amie nestled in between his strong legs. They watched together as the sun put on its glorious show. Patrick kissed the back of her neck and held his arms firmly beneath her breasts.

It was sad to see the sun dip below the horizon. *Goodbye, beautiful day.*

⌀

July 9, Thursday, Paul met with his probation officer, Chip Hammond. He was a good ten years younger than Paul and had also graduated from Salisbury University. His dull hazel eyes, doughy skin color, limp brown hair, and gaunt build added to his burned-out look as a probation officer. *Are you kidding me? Let me buy you a Big Mac and steak fries to put some meat on those bones.*

Chip had set up a quick ice-breaking meeting at 5:30 p.m. in Paul's one-bedroom apartment to go over some preliminary details and promised it wouldn't last more than half an hour. During the brief visit, Chip verified that Paul did indeed live at that address.

Chip said, "My visits in the future typically won't be real long...maybe an hour at the most." Paul nodded his head. "Do you have any questions or concerns you want to ask me today?"

"Not any that I can think of," said Paul.

Chip asked if Paul was still employed at Implant Products Inc., and Paul said he was. Chip said, "Don't be surprised if I show up there one day, and I may do an unscheduled visit to your home one time."

Oh, I'm shaking in my shoes. Paul offered him a Coke, which he declined. *How about some potatoes and rice, skinny fella?*

Chip said, "Give me the names of the people who live in the apartment next to you and across the hall."

"Why?" asked Paul.

"I need to ascertain if they may be negatively or positively influencing your chances of completing your probation period."

What are you, my mother? "They're nice neighbors. You don't have to be concerned about them," said Paul, but he surrendered their names to him.

"May I have a quick tour of your apartment?" asked Chip. "I'd like to look inside your refrigerator, if you don't mind." Chip searched the premises for illegal substances and items that could violate Paul's probation, such as hidden guns. Paul willingly let him do as he asked.

"Why did you want to search my fridge?" asked Paul.

"Most misdemeanors have a 'do not consume alcohol' condition."

Paul rolled his eyes. *Scrawny little punk. Who does he think he is, inspecting my fridge?*

As promised, their first visit was a short one, lasting about thirty minutes. They set up a mutually-agreed-upon date for their next meeting. Before leaving, Chip wrote down the time of arrival and departure, what had been discussed and observed, and a basic physical description of Paul's apartment, including a description of his company car and his black Ford F-150 truck.

Paul inhaled deeply when Chip walked out his apartment door. *What a relief.* Paul had paid his fines and was so glad he didn't have to serve a jail sentence. Being on probation was a huge obstacle, though. It didn't seem fair. He was glad the stalking of Amie wasn't introduced at the hearing by someone. He had kept that information from his lawyer, Jim Reynolds, but found out later that Reynolds had done his homework. He knew about Amie's filed police reports. *Shrewd attorney.*

The following day, Paul continued to look for houses in and around Ocean Pines. His desired house had to be in an isolated spot, inaccessible to nosy neighbors and the like. He found two more secluded houses that fit the bill. One was more remote than the other.

And of course, when the opportunity lent itself, Paul kept a vigilant eye on Amie.

CHAPTER 8

Amie called Cici to check on her. "How's it going?" asked Amie.

"I just got back from the doctor, and I had an ultrasound. We couldn't wait to be surprised. We're going to have a girl," said Cici.

"Wow! That's super, Cici. Is Joe happy?"

"He's ecstatic. In fact, he was so happy, he went out to buy a pink onesie at Carter's," said Cici. "We're both excited about getting the bedroom ready ahead of time."

"Only about four months to go?" asked Amie.

"About that, and no longer, I hope. Gotta think of some names now."

They chatted a little while longer, and then Amie had to end their conversation to show an open house. She drove to the north side of Ocean Pines and onto Clubhouse Lane, near the Ocean Pines Golf Course. She pulled her car around on a circular driveway and parked in front of a Cape Cod house. Pine trees and dogwoods grew in front of the circular driveway and obscured the front entrance to the house. A narrow canal ran along the left side of the home and widened at the rear. The clapboard house had a great view from the screened-in back porch and large deck, but the Cape Cod was old and needed quite a bit of updating.

Amie opened the lockbox. The house smelled musty when she stepped inside. Once inside the foyer, she rummaged inside her purse. She took out her lipstick spray and slipped it into the pocket of her blazer. *Just in case.*

The owner of the house, Mr. Ralph Martin, was a widower. He was ready to sell now that his wife was gone. Amie greeted him when she saw him staring out the smeared window of the back kitchen door. Amie was surprised that he was still in the house.

"Are you staying during the open house?" Amie asked. "I didn't realize you'd still be here."

"I'm not staying. I'll go out for a little while," he said.

"I see you removed all the photos in the living room. Are you going to take down the wallpaper in the bathroom and kitchen?"

"I don't know," said the widower. "I kind of like it. My wife did too."

"What about painting the dark paneling white? Don't you think that would brighten it up a little, like I suggested?" asked Amie.

"Not sure. Let's see what happens today," he said.

Won't have much interest today on this one. Needs too much work for the price he insists on.

Amie gave tours to two couples. One couple lingered longer than the other. Not a good turnout in two hours. None of them expressed any real interest. They could have been nosy neighbors. With a languid sigh, Amie began to pack up her brochures and grabbed her purse and keys. Before she reached the front door, widower man came charging inside. He was wide-eyed and pointed toward the front door.

"Mrs. McCombe, your car!"

"My car? What do you mean, Mr. Martin?"

"Come outside. Look at it!" She ran out front to the circular driveway.

In bright, bold red letters, the word *BITCH* was sprayed on both sides of her Saab. Amie called 911 to report the graffiti on her car. Again the police dusted for fingerprints, and again, Amie filed a police report.

⚵

Cici wanted to choose the right name for their baby girl. At breakfast that morning, she and Crabbe sipped their coffee and decided to search the internet for names of girls after eating. Joe Crabbe finished loading the dishes in the dishwasher, and Cici headed toward their computer.

"Joe, come in here so we can decide on some names for the baby. I'm seeing Amie later, so let's do it now." Joe eventually walked into their den and sat next to Cici. "How about Mary Caroline Crabbe?" Cici asked Joe.

"It sounds nice," he said.

"Or do you like something different, like Apple or North?"

"Of course not. How about Steamy. Steamy Crabbe." He laughed.

"Oh come on, Joe. Be real," said Cici. "How about Savannah Ann Crabbe?"

"No, they'll nickname her Sac. How about Sandy? Sandy Crabbe or Shelly Crabbe," said Joe. They both laughed. Their eyes searched the internet.

"It's hard to think of a name that goes with Crabbe. What was your mom's middle name?" asked Cici.

"Alison," said Crabbe.

"I like that one a lot. Would you like our baby to have your mother's name?" asked Cici.

"Let's consider it," said Crabbe.

⚜

Amie and Patrick both agreed it was time to ditch the Saab. That Saturday morning, July 18, they drove to Salisbury to look at new cars. They couldn't get much for Amie's Saab, so Amie donated it. She was happy with her purchase of a yellow Mini Cooper with a black convertible top and couldn't wait to take a leisure drive in it. Patrick had to go to his office to check on a case, and Amie told him she wanted to see if Cici wanted to go to lunch.

Amie called Cici, and she jumped at the chance to ride in Amie's new car and eat at Phillip's Crab House. Amie pulled into Cici's stone driveway. Cici rushed outside before Amie had a chance to get out of her car. "I was watching for you. Wow. It's adorable."

"Thanks," said Amie. "I thought I'd miss my Saab, but this one is so cute. I love it. It's me."

Cici slid into the passenger seat, strapped herself in, and brushed her hand across the dashboard. "It's really a cool car, Amie."

She noticed Amie's lipstick mace spray in the center console. "You haven't mentioned it, but has Paul bothered you since the graffiti incident?"

"No, but I'm not letting my guard down," said Amie.

"You'd better not. Today and tonight you can keep your mind off him, and we'll have fun. Joe will pick you guys up at 7:00 p.m. and then we'll head to Freeman Stage," said Cici.

"Can't wait to see the Eagles tonight," said Amie. "I love going there and enjoying concerts under the open sky." She sped along in her convertible on Coastal Highway, watching her speedometer. Amie slowed down and pulled into the restaurant's parking lot.

"I'm ordering a crab cake," said Cici.

"Me too." Amie found a parking spot and didn't put the top up before getting out of the car.

"What about Rayne?" asked Cici.

"I think the weatherman said it's not supposed to," said Amie.

"I mean the name for my baby girl," said Cici.

"Oh," she laughed. "Hmmm. It's different. I like it," said Amie.

Inside Phillip's Crab House, they were seated immediately. After ordering drinks, they discussed girls' names and ordered crab cakes and coleslaw.

After lunch, Amie drove back home leaving the top down. With her golden hair whipping in the wind and her head bobbing, she turned on the radio full blast and sang, along with Gloria Gaynor, "I Will Survive" all the way down Coastal Highway.

⊰⊱

A little before the concert, two men walked into the ticket office at Freeman Stage and asked whether any tickets were still available to see the Eagles perform. When the front-desk employee told them the show was sold out, the men grew agitated. One of the men, wearing a red T-shirt and flip-flops, asked what would happen if he and his friend jumped the fence.

The employee clasped his throat with his hand and in a shaky voice said, "Security will remove you and have you arrested."

"Well, what would happen if we were to jump the fence with guns?" T-shirt man said.

The employee stood bug-eyed. He felt his heartbeat increasing. To pacify them, he handed the two men a list of upcoming events. They then left. Immediately after they were gone, the front-desk employee ran over to the event organizers and the band to inform them of the warning by the one man. Due to the alleged threats, the show was canceled one hour before the Eagles were to perform. State and local authorities were notified also.

When Patrick, Amie, Cici, and Joe arrived at Freeman Stage, they were so disappointed when they heard about the show's cancelation. At least they were told they could get their money refunded. Joe turned his car around, and they all decided to have dinner at Catch 54 in Fenwick Island, Delaware.

After Joe dropped Amie and Patrick off at their house in Ocean Pines, Amie said, "Well, it was disappointing not to see the Eagles, but at least we did have a nice dinner. Patrick, we better search the house. Don't you think?"

Patrick nodded and said he definitely agreed. Even though their house was a rancher, it was a spacious 2,700-foot home with a two-car garage. Patrick led the search with Amie trailing behind him, her hand firmly holding on to the waistband of his pants.

"Check the powder room," Amie said. They found no poop, no graffiti, no flowers, and no unwelcome place settings. After the search was completed and all was well, Patrick then inspected the camera film. It revealed that no one had approached the house.

There was news the next day from Patrick that they caught the men who had terrorized the ticket man at Freeman Stage. Patrick told Amie that he and Joe learned that T-shirt man had turned himself in after the local media released photos of him. He was charged and released on $20,000 bail, and he surrendered the name of his partner to the authorities. They arrested his friend that evening.

⚑

Monday, while Amie munched on grapes and cheese at her desk, Mr. Martin, the widower and owner of the Cape Cod house, interrupted her snacking. His name registered on her iPhone as it pinged. "Mrs. McCombe—"

"Please call me Amie, Mr. Martin," she said.

"Any news on my house? Have you had any calls? Any interest?"

"Not yet, Mr. Martin. But how badly do you want to sell it?"

"Right away. The house is too much for me to take care of at my age, and you know I have memories here that make me sad."

"I think we can sell it if you are willing to let me make some changes. I can stop by later this afternoon, and we can discuss what we can do," Amie said. *Don't want to hurt his feelings, but his house needs some help. Sweet old man. He needs to lower the price.*

"I'll do anything you say. I guess I should have listened to you in the first place," Mr. Martin said.

Amie told him that she would like to stage his house. "Can you store some of your furniture? We need to clear some pieces out and make your rooms seem larger."

"Actually, I'm not taking any of it with me. The kids can take what they want. I only need my bed, my armchair, and my TV. My name is closer to the top of the list to move into the retirement home I've chosen. They told me I might have an apartment there next month."

"That's good news. You do have some very nice furniture. Let's see what your children select, and you need to decide which pieces you may need for your apartment aside from just a bed and a chair," said Amie. "I think we should paint the dark-paneled wall white, and also the whole first floor could use a couple of coats as well. It would really brighten your home up. We need to declutter and strip off the wallpaper. I suggest you pack away or get rid of most of your knickknacks."

"Like I said, Amie, I'll do anything to sell it as quickly as possible."

"I know of a reasonable painter. But there's one more thing. We need to lower your asking price $10,000," said Amie.

"I had a feeling you would suggest that. I'll do it," he said.

A week later, the painter came and freshened up the living room, dining room, foyer, and kitchen. Mr. Martin's children took what they wanted. They carried keepsakes, tables, pictures, bric-a-brac, various kitchen items, twin beds, a recliner, and a love seat, and they cleaned out the garage of Mr. Martin's numerous tools. The rest went to Goodwill.

Amie arrived at the end of the week and was surprised at how the changes in the house, with less clutter and white walls, improved its interior, almost as if it were magic. Amie went to work staging the home. She asked Mr. Martin to keep the classic round-arm sofa and two small club chairs in the living room. The neutral beige colors looked appealing with the white walls and brick fireplace. He consigned the breakfront and buffet, and Amie wanted the expensive wood-grained dining room table to stay. She set it with brand-new placemats, white dishes, and Mr. Martin's silverware. Mr. Martin hung one mirror above the fireplace in the living room and hammered one nail in the dining room for an abstract painting Amie gave him to make the room pop. Amie removed all the outdated curtains on the windows. Plenty of sunlight brightened the home now. She cleared the kitchen countertops of all unnecessary items. The upstairs, she didn't stage. Mr. Martin agreed to hire a professional maid service to do an initial deep cleaning of his entire home.

Two days later Amie wanted to hear Mr. Martin's opinion of his new surroundings. "Well, what do you think?" she asked him as he stood there looking dumbfounded.

"I'm impressed. What a difference it makes. You were right, Amie," he said, smiling.

Three and a half weeks later, they had a buyer for the house.

CHAPTER 9

Monday, July 27, Paul's meeting with his probation officer was considered his first official monthly hour-long meeting. Chip was there at his apartment at 5:00 p.m. Paul arrived at his apartment at 5:15 p.m. after a full day's work. Chip was waiting in the hallway.

"Sorry to keep you waiting," said Paul as he turned the corner from the elevator.

"No problem," said Chip. "You know you have a choice where we can meet. We can meet at my office each month instead of your apartment if you like."

Paul said his apartment was fine.

They sat down in the living room. "Still working at Implant Products?" asked Chip. "Sorry; I have to keep tabs on your employment status."

"Yes, still there. I understand you have to check," said Paul.

"What do you do when you're not working, Paul? You look fit. Do you work out?"

"I swim laps over at the fitness center several times a week," said Paul.

"Now I can see why you look like you keep in shape. That's great. Anything else?"

"That exercise keeps me pretty busy, believe me."

"Are you in a relationship with anyone?"

"Nothing serious. I like this one doctor over at Peninsula General. She's a bit of a tease, though. A big flirt. Don't think she's interested in hooking up with a salesman, though," said Paul. "I date women, but none have really pushed my buttons yet."

"Have you ever been in a serious relationship?" asked Chip.

"Yeah, several years ago, but we broke up." *If he only knew how much I want her back with me.*

"Was it mutual?" asked Chip.

"Oh yeah," said Paul. *He's getting a little too personal now.*

"I'm familiar with your case. You really harbor a lot of resentment for this one guy, Patrick McCombe, don't you?"

"I can't help it."

"You need to move on and abandon those feelings. How long have you held revenge for this guy…Patrick?"

"Many years," said Paul. He explained to Chip more about why he was so angry at Patrick.

"I'd like you to join an anger management group at the hospital."

"No, Chip. I don't like to discuss my personal business or feelings in front of people. It's just not me. I don't mind talking about it with you, though."

"It could help you to control and channel your feelings in other ways. But I hear you. I have a video on anger management that you can see, since you prefer not to join a group."

"That sounds much better," said Paul.

"There's one condition, though. We'll watch it together and have a discussion about it afterward."

"Fine," said Paul. They conversed more, and then they began to wrap up their session, setting the date for their next meeting.

Chip glanced at his watch and said, "I'll let you have your dinner. See you on August 10."

Paul had a restless sleep that night. When he eventually fell back to sleep, he dreamed that Patrick nabbed him as he was trying to flee with Amie after breaking into their house again. In his dream, patrol cars were everywhere outside Amie's house; Chip Hammond was shaking his head and finger at him, and Patrick said he was going to put him in jail forever. Paul woke up, turned over, and lay there awake for another hour. *Gotta get back to sleep. Just a stupid dream.*

On Wednesday, July 28, Paul transferred some cash from his deferred annuity fund into his regular checking account. He was very interested in a property that was going to be auctioned off on August 7 by Coastal Auctioneers. The house on the property was very secluded. A long dirt road surrounded by a tunnel of trees led up to the house. The trees' branches on either side of the narrow road extended overhead, joining together and forming an arch that opened up to a small clearing ahead. The clearing, covered in pine needles and cones, was situated in front of the house. Thick woods bordered the back of the house, and behind the dense trees was the river.

On August 6, Paul put on his boots after a storm had hit the day before and explored the one-acre timbered grounds where the house was. He peered through the maze of trees in the woods that overlooked the water. The house was tiny, neglected, and deserted, but the one-acre lot and the sur-rounding area was a bonus.

When Friday, August 7, rolled around, Paul gassed up his car, had a cashier's check made out to himself, and set out to go to the house auction being held 1.7 miles from Ocean Pines. The house was located off Showell School Road, deep in a wooden area near Windmill Creek, a stream that emp-tied into the Shingle Landing Prong. On the other side of the stream was the River Run Golf Course.

The house being auctioned off was set back 150 yards from Shingle Landing Prong. It was unkempt from the out-side, so the inside must have been just as bad. Paul knew he was buying it as is, but the auction provided an opportunity for a great value. On the side of the house an old oil tank jut-ted up against the yellow siding, and Paul noticed he would have to walk through a screened-in porch to get to the front door. A tilted, shabby potting shed and wooden shanty cov-ered in vines were on the property not too far from the house.

Paul had done his research on the property and sought independent advice from a real estate attorney. He researched the estimated market value of the property, how much the borrower might have owed on the mortgage, and whether there were any liens against the property. He also had the real estate attorney run a title search.

Paul arrived an hour before the bidding started at noon, scouting the area again. He really wanted the house, even though it looked as if a wolf could blow it down with one puff. He liked that it was near the Saint Martin's River and provided good bass and bluegill fishing.

Paul had arrived around the same time as the auctioneer. The auctioneer had squinty eyes. His wrinkled, leathery skin on his cheeks and forehead had to be from being in the sun too much. Good thing he was quite tall, so that the crowd could spot him well. Paul saw a few people asking questions and registering near the auctioneer and his assistants. After the people registered, they were handed a bidding packet. Having preregistered, Paul had not gotten one. He walked over to the auctioneer, introduced himself, and politely asked him for a packet.

"Thank you for coming," the auctioneer said to Paul. "I'm Walter Crane." They shook hands.

"Pleasure to meet you." Paul walked around the house and back to the front. He then stood among a small crowd facing the auctioneer and his team. Paul overheard a conversation between a couple who seemed interested in the property. The bald man was of short stature and had a prominent mustache above his thick lips. His wife was a long-legged, tall woman with tousled mink-brown hair and a trim body. Her left large finger showed off a stunning two-carat solitaire diamond engagement ring and gold wedding band.

"This is a great deal if we can get it," the short man said. "The house is in lousy condition, though."

"Ari, look at all the trees. We have to knock a lot of them down to clear it more, and that will cost a fortune," said his wife.

"And we'll bulldoze the fleapit down, Susan. More money to shell out," said Ari.

"And also the shed and shack over there," his wife said. "Oh, there's our contractor. He just arrived. I'm glad we made an appointment with the auctioneer before this to inspect the inside," said his wife. "I don't want to go in there again."

"Yea, it's a useless dump, and I didn't tell you, but I saw mouse droppings in the kitchen," said Ari.

Their contractor spotted them and waved.

"Hi, Kyle."

Kyle shook Ari's hand and nodded to Susan.

"So *this* is the place you two want," Kyle said.

"We'd like to knock the three buildings down and build our country house over there." She pointed.

"Do you think we have plenty of room on the property for cages and pens for the animals?"

He scanned the acre, nodding his head. "I can do what you want. We have plenty of space to build your new house and animal pens. Your idea of having a place for injured and lost animals is an act of humanity. There aren't many people who would do that, Mr. and Mrs. Dillon," Kyle said.

The auctioneer was busy with three people, answering questions. Paul thought that the auction would attract a number of realtors, professional investors, and builders. He shifted a little closer to two men who were chatting and eavesdropped on their conversation while he pretended to read his bidding packet. One man was speaking to a home inspector about the structure of the house and asking him about the heating and plumbing. Paul watched others as they were touring the site. About a dozen people were gathered in front of the auctioneer's stand. The hour went by quickly, and the auctioneer finally shouted that it was time to start the bidding.

"Welcome, everyone. Coastal Auctioneers is auctioning off a nice piece of property here today. We're fortunate to have pleasant weather and a good crowd for the bidding. You people are pretty smart to be here today, because this is the fastest way to buy real estate. I hope you've done your homework on this property. If you haven't read your packet, which I strongly urge you to do, you will find out that you are bidding on this house, which was built in 1968. If you haven't had a chance to inspect the inside of the house, it consists of a living room, two bedrooms, one bath, and an eat-in kitchen. It's a one-story aluminum siding home on a wooded lot with a total square footage of 760 square feet inside. It has a private well and septic tank. The property is in fee simple and is sold free and clear of liens. It's composed of approximately one acre of land and is sold in as-is condition. The asking price was $89,000 on the internet real estate sites, if you've done your research. The family took the house off the market a while back and now wants to sell the property as soon as possible since no action occurred on it for months. This is an estate sale auction. The owner passed away, and the property is being sold for the estate of that person. An attorney is present acting as the personal representative for the family. A $5,000 cashier's check deposit is required to open the bidding. The balance is to be paid in cash at settlement, which shall take place in forty-five days. I think most of you showed me that you have the required deposit to qualify to bid. If you don't have that, you can't bid."

One lady ran up to him, apologized, and showed him her check. He paused and examined the check. Crane shook his head and smiled at her.

"The process will be fast, so pay attention. Bids will be made orally. No need to raise your hand. Any bidding amount is acceptable. The highest bidder will take possession of the property. Any questions? Everyone ready?" The auctioneer looked at his watch. "OK, I will now solicit bids for the property."

At the end of the auctioneer's announcements, Paul felt his heart pumping fast. *This is exciting.* He leaned against a tree trunk and made sure the auctioneer had a good view of him.

"Five thousand dollars," said a voice behind Paul.

"Five thousand five hundred," someone said.

"Seven thousand," said Ari.

"Eight thousand," said Paul.

"Ten thousand," shouted a woman.

"Fifteen thousand," said Ari.

The bidding reached into the $20,000 range. Paul heard a woman's voice say, "I'm out."

"Twenty-five thousand," said the couple.

"Thirty thousand," said the voice behind Paul.

Paul kept eye contact with the auctioneer. "Thirty-five thousand," he said and heard the couple bid the same amount a millisecond later.

"Wait—we said thirty-five thousand first," said the couple, Ari and Susan Dillon, waving their hands at the same time to get the auctioneer's attention.

Paul said, "No, I'm afraid you didn't. You shouted it a second after I did."

"No, we didn't! You're mistaken," the couple said to Paul.

"I have the bid," said Paul.

The auctioneer finally said, "All right, let's stop this dispute. I'm to decide who said the bid first." He paused and said, "I'm 100 percent certain the gentleman leaning against the tree did say it first."

Ari's eyebrows pulled together, and his face reddened. "Some gentleman. Are you kidding me?" Susan just shook her head.

The auctioneer said, "Let's move on. The last bid is thirty-five thousand dollars. Any more bids?"

There was silence. "Going once…going twice. Sold," said the auctioneer.

The small group clapped as Paul smiled. The husband, Ari, and his wife, Susan, gave Paul the foulest look and trudged away with their contractor, Kyle. Paul walked over to the auctioneer, who congratulated him. The auctioneer said, "You really did beat them on that bid. I don't know why they stopped bidding. These clashes sometimes happen."

"I guess so," said Paul. He endorsed the check over to the auctioneer.

"You will be notified of the settlement date. You may want to select an attorney for the closing," said the auctioneer.

Paul couldn't wait to obtain his certificate of title.

After the auction, Paul went to a consignment and thrift shop on Route 50 near Berlin. He made a checklist of items he thought he'd need to furbish his little shack. He could possibly use some of the furniture already in his apartment, but the rest he'd consign. He didn't want to touch any of his mother's furniture and antiques taken from her now-closed antique shop. He had put them all in storage. Paul decided to discard the things that were left inside the tiny house, except for a walnut kitchen table and two matching chairs that were still in good condition. He would wait until he moved in before he purchased items for the house. He planned to hire a painter to brighten the inside. Maybe he'd paint the walls himself. He'd also hire an inspector to examine the plumbing, the air-conditioners fastened in the windows, the septic tank, and the well.

What a quiet, secluded place to keep Amie with me. No one will know we're there together, building our new life in the woods. We'll have it all to ourselves. I know I can make her happy and rekindle her feelings for me while I convince her that Patrick is not the man for her. Eventually we'll construct a beautiful home on the lot that's lovelier than the one she's in now.

CHAPTER 10

Paul yawned as he watched the video on anger management with Chip during the meeting on Monday, August 10, with his probation officer. "You bored?" asked Chip. "You've been yawning a couple of times."

"No, no. I had a long day at work. A lot of calls. That's all," said Paul. *What a monotonous video.*

"Well, it's almost over," said Chip. "I hope you benefited from seeing some of the techniques." Chip looked at the time remaining on the video. "OK, two minutes to go, and then we can discuss what strategies you think could help you manage your anger better."

He yawned again and blinked his eyes a few times. The video finally stopped. "Why don't you start?" asked Paul.

"OK, Paul, do you acknowledge that you have a problem with anger?" asked Chip.

"Yes, I have a lot of built-up anger," he said.

"What do you think about keeping a hostility log?" said Chip.

I'll say anything to get this over with. "Yeah, I can try it," said Paul. "It seems like a good idea."

"Great. Next time you have an anger episode, monitor the trigger for it. When you start to feel angry, try deep breathing and count to twenty before you respond. You could also try meditation. Next month when we meet, I'd like to see your log," said Chip. "And here's a brochure on controlling your anger and aggression and suggestions how to set up your log."

Oh boy, I can't wait. He flipped through the pages. "Good," Paul said, nodding his head. "It looks like there are a lot of techniques I can use, but I'm hoping I don't have any anger issues."

"Well, if you do, try one of those techniques, and we'll see what works best for you. You also might be interested in trying yoga."

"No, I don't think so, Chip," said Paul.

A knock on the door interrupted them. "I'd better answer that," said Paul.

"Of course."

When Paul opened the door, his coworker Matt Brooks stood there, one hand on his hip.

"Hey, buddy," said Matt. He glanced over Paul's shoulder at Chip on the sofa.

"Oh, that's my neighbor Chip," said Paul. "He was just leaving."

Matt said, "Tim and I are meeting over at Hooper's Tap House. I stopped by hoping you could join us. There are rumors going around at work. We need to talk," said Matt.

"Rumors?" asked Paul.

"Yep. Can you come?" Matt glanced at Chip again. "We can get a bite to eat if you're not busy or haven't eaten already."

"No, I haven't had dinner yet." Paul looked at his watch. "It's a little past 6:00 p.m."

"I didn't mean to interrupt you and your neighbor," said Matt.

Chip rose from the sofa. "I was just about to leave." He gathered his video and brochure and stuffed his papers inside a case and latched it.

Paul turned around. "Chip, I'll call you, and we can discuss the matter some more," he said.

"You bet," said Chip, and he left.

Matt's brow furrowed and his hands and arms opened, forming a questioning gesture.

Paul saw Matt's curious look and said, "He came over, and we were discussing that there's a possibility our apartments are going to become condominiums. Some of the neighbors are protesting." said Paul. "I'll get my keys, and I'll meet you over there."

"Sounds good," said Matt.

Never want Matt to find out I'm on probation.

⚔

The guys gathered around a circular high-top table at Hooper's Tap House and ordered chicken wings, steamed shrimp, and beer. The bar was dark, loud, and busy.

When their orders came, Paul sipped his beer and cleared his throat. Tim sneaked a peek at their waitress's butt as she strode back toward the bar, swinging her hips. "So what's going on?" asked Paul.

"Well, it seems that there's a rumor that some of us are going to be laid off," said Matt.

"What?" asked Paul. "How do you know that?"

"Don't repeat this," said Matt. "But the CEO's secretary, Kim Archer, told Tim in confidence."

"That sexy broad?" said Paul. "Heard she sleeps around. I thought she and the CEO had a thing going on." Paul stared at Tim. "So she told you about the layoffs? No kidding."

Tim nodded and said, "I'm sure it's pretty accurate. She wouldn't tell me if it weren't true. She doesn't know any more than that."

"So, you know her pretty well, huh?" said Paul.

"You could say that," said Tim. He smirked.

"Women can't keep their hands off you," said Matt. The guys knew women were attracted to his well-defined muscles and sturdy frame.

"The CEO is calling a meeting tomorrow morning for everyone," said Tim.

"How come I didn't know about any of this?" asked Paul.

"You were on a sales call at a hospital. We both just found out about the meeting at the end of the day like everyone else," said Matt.

"Are they making cuts because Implant Products isn't profitable?" asked Paul. "Do you know if our revenues were far below last quarter?"

"I doubt it. I can't afford to be laid off," said Matt. "I've got to take care of my three kids. They're all slated to go to college. Plus, I have a huge mortgage. This will kill me if they let me go."

"Let's not be overly rash. Let's see what happens. We may not be affected at all," said Tim. "It's either that we're undergoing restructuring or, maybe, downsizing. And it could be only temporary. Hope it's not that we're going out of business."

"Yeah, the economy isn't real great right now," said Matt, scratching his royale beard.

"Stop being Debbie Downers, guys. I guess we'll find out first thing in the morning," Paul said as he chewed on his barbequed chicken wing. *They won't lay me off. I'm too good at what I do. I've gotten raises and bonuses. They need me. My sales record is better than Matt's and Tim's.*

᚛

The next morning, on Tuesday, August 11, Paul, wearing a lightweight polo shirt and tan pants, arrived early at Implant Products and headed straight toward the sales office to speak to his sales manager, Byron Walker.

"Good morning," Paul said with a slight smile. "Hot outside," he said, fanning himself with his hand.

"Yeah, supposed to be in the nineties," said Byron.

"Glad I caught you before the meeting. There's rumors on the grapevine about the purpose of the meeting. I'll come right to the point. Should I be concerned about being laid off?"

Walker blinked his eyes several times and said, "You have nothing to worry about. We had better get downstairs to the meeting."

"OK, thanks." Paul walked out of his office, and from Byron's body language, Paul would bet he was lying and was uncomfortable talking about it. Paul headed toward the large conference room, where his coworkers were entering the main doors. Some of the coworkers, who were taking their seats, were secretaries, receptionists, maintenance staff, orthopedic product salesmen (seven, to be exact), two VPs, three departments heads, technicians, two engineers, an accounting manager, the customer service rep, programmers, the human resources director, a senior project manager, and the quality control inspector. The CEO walked in with Byron Walker. Paul, Matt, and Tim sat together. Sober faces filled the conference room. Approximately thirty-five were seated in the room.

"Hello, everyone," said the CEO, Winston Price. He raised his plump hand in a wave gesture. His poor posture caused his shoulders to droop. Even so, he was a sixty-eight-year-old stocky, bald man of six feet in height. His eyes were red-rimmed, appearing as if he had been crying.

"I've called this meeting abruptly, but that's because things have been moving very quickly around here. As you know, I have owned this small company for over thirty-nine years, and Implant Products, I'm proud to say, has provided an opportunity for people to live a better life. This industry has integrity with all our relationships and believes in service before self. We represent health-care products of the highest quality and the finest design. As you are well aware, because Implant Products is a small, privately owned company, it causes a lot more work for all of my employees, and believe me, I've appreciated all your efforts. Our accomplishments and services have been noteworthy and have not gone unnoticed. I've called you all here today because I have been offered a generous buyout from Ortho-Designs in Dover, Delaware. I will be leaving the company, and I am sure you realize this venture will have an impact on you. Because there is a duplication of positions, many of you will be laid off. Some of you will receive a handsome severance package and others cash bonuses. I am giving you notice today that most of you will be terminated August 31." Murmuring could be heard throughout the room. "I realize this is not happy news, and I am very sorry for that. For those of you who have signed a noncompete agreement, it will take effect the day of your dismissal. Some of you will remain, but as soon as I finalize things with Ortho-Designs, I will notify those who will be keeping their positions. Again, thank you for your service. If you have any questions, our VP, David, will be happy to answer them for you."

Everyone turned to one another, and loud talking filled the room. Price extended his arm, welcoming the vice president as he drew closer to the front of the room. Winston Price then left the podium.

David Crawford stepped behind the podium. Employees in the auditorium were suddenly quiet. He cleared his throat and said, "I know our caring CEO was not happy to apprise some of you that your jobs are in jeopardy." He continued to speak and began answering questions from the group.

Paul had faintly heard what his leader, Price, had said about his reasons for termination. Sitting there, he felt as if he were in a dense fog. He glanced at Matt next to him and tried to keep calm, taking a deep breath. Paul, Matt, and Tim left their seats during David Crawford's discourse and decided to exit the small auditorium and gather in the men's room.

"Son of a bitch," said Tim. "I'm sure we'll be the ones to be laid off. They have plenty of salespeople in Ortho-Designs. They're huge."

Paul said, "Winston Price must have gotten one hell of a golden parachute."

"Well, wouldn't you take it and leave if you were his age and in his position?" asked Tim. He turned toward Matt. "Wha—"

Matt brushed past Tim, knocked into his shoulder, and darted over to the urinal and vomited into it.

⚖

Employees at Implant Products could stop sitting on eggshells, because when Wednesday morning, August 12, rolled around, the bomb dropped. Paul learned he was part of the layoff. In fact, 50 percent of the employees found out they were going to be dismissed. Paul was told he had three weeks to gather whatever belongings he needed to take with him.

Paul knew the CEO's intent wasn't malicious, but it sure felt that way to him. *Feels like a burning slap to my face. This sudden dismissal was inappropriate.*

Paul, Tim, and Matt met for lunch at Burger King and discussed the situation.

"I'm not even hungry. God, I feel so humiliated," said Tim. "Can't believe we've been shitcanned. I'm comfortable and familiar with my job. I'm going to miss the challenges, the milestones, the inside jokes, happy-hour times at the bar and grill, and, of course, you guys," said Tim.

Matt said, shaking his head, "I can't believe all my years of dedication to this job are now coming to an end. It sucks."

"I didn't fathom this would hit me as hard as it does. I have to give up the leased company car, my laptop, and mobile phone. Guys, it doesn't mean we weren't good performers. Hell, remember GM reduced their staff down to forty-seven thousand people. I can't let myself think I'm a failure," said Paul.

"We're not losers, Paul. Geez, but what a massive layoff. I was expecting maybe 25 percent of the people would be let go," said Matt.

"Yeah, we don't deserve this. The company was very sales driven. As long as we created good numbers, I thought we were fine," said Paul. "I feel as if my contribution to the company was deemed inconsequential in the end."

"Me too," said Tim. "But I guess it was up to the guys in Dover to replace our positions. It'll feel awkward telling my family and friends at the gym I've been let go."

"And we have to be out of here at the end of the month. That was too abrupt a dismissal," said Matt.

"Well, it beats hanging around here any longer. I'd like to get out of this place as soon as possible. Hate when they say it's not personal; it's only business," said Paul.

"I still say he should have given us more notice. You and Tim are lucky. You don't have a wife and three kids to support. I'm going to have to start working on my resume," said Matt. "Maybe I'll consider a different career path. Maybe I'll be happier in a slightly different job."

Paul said, "It's like the Game of Life."

Tim patted Matt on the back. "You'll be OK. We'll prevail. At least we're getting a nice severance package and stock options," said Tim.

"Yeah, but we haven't received the package yet." Paul stood up to leave, and he gulped the remainder of his Diet Pepsi down. "Come on; let's go."

Tim said, "Hey, Paul, since you don't want them, can I have the rest of your french fries?"

Paul woke up at 3:00 a.m. and was unable to fall back to sleep because the realization hit him that he would be an unemployed and a noncontributing member of society. *It's not my fault. Can't help but hate Winston Price.*

Ever since being told about the layoff, Paul had been having a difficult time accepting it. He went into a dark state of mind. *Will anyone hire me?* He felt worthless. At work, he didn't care about calling on his customers. He only went to the clinics or hospitals if they needed a product. He spent as little time as possible at work and mostly drove around. He left earlier than the rest of the employees. Fatigue and headaches were a common occurrence. But Paul did do one good thing that pulled him out of the doldrums. He sought help from the Employee Assistance Program at work. He vented his feelings to a woman, Beth Owens, in charge. She was very understanding and helpful.

"I'm not in a good place. I feel trapped and unable to do anything about the way I feel," Paul said. "I'm spending more energy on worrying than anything else."

Ms. Owens talked extensively to Paul about coping with his situation and gave him rock-solid advice. "You're not alone," she said. "This has been traumatic for most of the employees here. You seem to me that you're strong enough to eventually accept this and face the problem. It will pass," she said.

It will pass? Says who? She still has her job. I'm the loser, not her.

⊶

Sunday evening, August 16, Paul assessed his finances. *I have the proceeds from my mother's house, my 401(k) is decent, and I have stock in Apple that's done very well. Plus, I have the severance package. I'll have no mortgage on the new house, but I'll have to buy a new car, and I'll probably keep the truck for a while.*

Paul decided to file for unemployment sometime when the first week of September rolled around. He had to turn in his company car, and he had given notice to the landlord that he would not be renting his apartment after August 31. He thought about exploring other careers, like Matt had said. He would make arrangements to have his mail delivered to a PO box rather than to his house in the woods.

He called Chip and told him that it would be easier for him to have their monthly meetings at Chip's office, and Paul set the date when he would see him in September. He didn't want Chip to know he was deserting his apartment, leaving his job, and buying a new car. He'd sell his mother's Ford F-150 truck, which she had used in her antiquing business, and put the cash from that toward a new car. On September 1, he would begin living elsewhere. He'd rent a place in Ocean City for a few weeks before settlement on September 21 on his little house. After settlement, he'd have time to put some TLC into the house and keep an eye on Amie. That made him smile.

Paul, Matt, and Tim met at their usual Friday bar and grill for happy hour. A number of employees from Implant Products were also hanging loose at the bar. The three friends sat at a high-top table away from the rest of their coworkers.

Tim said, "I talked to the manager at the gym where I work out, and he offered me a position as a trainer if I want it. The salary sucks, but I could look for a decent sales job in the meantime, and Kim said I could move into her condo with her temporarily. Not sure if that's a good idea, though. I like my freedom too much. I should get a cheaper place to live and move into a one-bedroom apartment like you, Paul."

Paul nodded.

Matt said, "The next day after I heard about the buyout, I sent my resume to an orthopedic company in Baltimore that was advertising for a sales rep. We decided to put our house on the market. I'll need to find a well-paying job, and I doubt if I can find one here in Salisbury that pays as well as Implant Products. Sally's parents live in Annapolis, and she's fine with it if we have to move up there. And as luck would have it, the company called me yesterday to interview with them next week."

"Boy, that was fast. You're really rolling. That's great," said Paul. "But you'll be missed if you move to Baltimore, my buddy."

"Yeah, I know. I'll miss you guys too," said Matt. "But they haven't offered me the job yet. If the house sells, we can live with her parents until I find the right position with good pay. Sally can substitute teach and apply for a full-time teaching position when one becomes available."

"Oh, you'll get the job, with your good sales record and recommendations. But what about the noncompete?" asked Tim.

"I'm not worried about that. Most times, they don't go after you at all. Besides, I'll be far away from Implant Products. But I'd appreciate it if you didn't say anything to anyone about this if I'm offered the position," said Matt.

"Don't worry; we won't," said Paul. He and Tim clinked Matt's beer bottle. "To no more insecurity."

"What about you, Paul?" asked Matt.

"Well, I'll put feelers out there like you two have done." *That's all they need to know. Keeping my personal business to myself.*

"Sounds like we all have a plan," said Matt, and they clinked bottles again. "It's done. Game over. Onward and upward."

Paul received an avalanche of information about his severance package, COBRA options, and papers to be signed. His package paid him his full salary for one year. That gave him a huge sigh of relief. During this interim time, Beth Owens from the Employment Assistance Program advised Paul to do something that could relieve his stress, such as continuing his swimming laps. Ms. Owens knew that Paul enjoyed that type of exercise. That was fine, but his real enjoyment and passion was to observe Amie's comings and goings.

CHAPTER 11

On Sunday, August 23, Paul drove to the Valero gas station on Racetrack Road. After filling his truck's tank up with gas, he swerved out of the station and stopped at the red light at Cathell Road. He saw Patrick's SUV whiz by with Amie inside and turn left onto Racetrack Road. Paul followed them but kept three cars behind until they turned left again onto Ocean Gateway, which was Route 50. Paul stayed a reasonable distance back from them. Patrick and Amie turned right off of Route 50 and then made a left into a parking lot filled with cars. Paul pointed his truck toward the entrance to the lot. He watched them walk toward the end of the parking lot, where a restaurant was located near the inlet. Patrick and Amie circled around the side of the building holding hands.

Paul had to see Amie. He just couldn't keep away. What a special day.

"Grab that barstool," said Patrick. Amie and Patrick sat at the outdoor covered bar at Mickey Fins, located in the Ocean City Fishing Center. The outside bar had great marina views. Fishing trawlers and boats brought in their catches of the day. It was an exceptionally warm day. He and Amie washed down their appetizers of killer clams and mahi fingers with their tequila sunrises.

Amie said, "I'm so glad that Paul has a probation officer for a whole year. It may set him straight. If he does text me, he violates his probation, right?"

Patrick said, "Yes."

"What happens if he violates it?" asked Amie.

"It's up to the judge. He could spend some time in jail," said Paul.

"Good. I think it's great that he's being monitored."

"Let's change the subject and talk about something else," said Patrick.

"Agreed," said Amie.

They watched the boats cruising in the canal with their freshly caught fish. The fishermen brought in blue fin, croakers, flounder, and tuna. Patrick and Amie stood up in the bar overlooking the lower deck while the men unloaded the fish. "Wow, look at that tuna!" Amie said.

"That will be somebody's dinner tonight," said Patrick. The fisherman hauled up the yellowfin tuna on the scale to weigh it.

"Fifty-eight pounds," a man said. The crew gave a cheer.

"At the Ocean City Tuna Tournament back in July, they caught bigger ones than that. The winner got over $300,000," Patrick said.

"No way," said Amie. "Let's go next year to that tournament."

Saturday, August 29, Amie and Cici rode in Amie's yellow convertible to the outdoor farmers market, held in White Horse Park next to the fire house. They looked forward to getting some fresh produce and browsing the booths with crafts and jewelry.

"Cici, your baby bump is getting bigger," said Amie. "She must have grown some overnight."

"I know." Cici laughed. "Only two months to go. The doctor estimated my due date to be November 18."

"I can't wait," Amie said.

"Neither can I. My mom will fly out here the middle of November and stay with us for a couple of weeks."

"Great idea," said Amie.

"I haven't seen her since before Greg's trial," said Cici.

They stopped at the fresh produce booth, and Amie and Cici picked out corn, tomatoes, plums, acorn squash, and eggplant. "I'm going to fry that eggplant for tonight. Come over about sevenish," said Cici.

"We'll bring dessert," said Amie. She finished gathering her produce and set the items down on the counter. As she casually glanced across the way toward the next aisle beyond the booth, her face lost its color. The cashier diverted Amie's attention by telling her what she owed for her fruits and vegetables. Amie's hand shook as she dropped her change on the ground.

"What's wrong, Amie? You look like you've seen a ghost," said Cici.

"I think I just saw Paul over there."

"Where?" Cici asked as she looked in the direction Amie indicated. "He's not there now. Maybe it wasn't him."

Amie put her hand over her heart. "I need to collect myself. My heart skipped a beat," said Amie. She deeply inhaled and held her breath.

Cici squinted, glimpsing over at the next aisle. "I still don't see him, Amie. Maybe it was someone who looked like him," she said.

They finished paying for their purchases and walked toward the parking lot to go home. "Wait," Cici said. "I want to get that crab wind chime hanging over there in that booth. It'll look cute on our deck."

After Cici bought her wind chime, they headed back to Amie's convertible. The yellow Mini Cooper's top was down, which made it easy for them to set their brown paper bags on the back seat of the car. Amie started the engine and headed to Cici's house in south Ocean Pines. She dropped her friend off and headed home.

That evening, when Amie made herself comfortable on the couch in Cici and Joe's living room, she told Joe she thought she had seen Paul at the farmers market, looking straight at her. "Then when I looked again, he was gone."

"I didn't see anyone over in the next aisle that resembled him," Cici said.

Amie said, "Well, let's all be vigilant. If I see him near us, it's a violation of his probation, and Patrick told me he could go to jail." Amie's cell phone buzzed. It was Patrick texting her.

"Where *is* your husband? I thought he'd be here by now," said Cici.

"Patrick just texted me that he's on his way. He just finished closing a case and is coming back here now from Ocean City."

Patrick arrived fifteen minutes later. They heard the glass front storm door slam shut. "Sorry I'm late," he said.

"You look worn out, Patrick," said Cici.

"Yeah, I should. I had an interesting evening," he said.

"I hope not another jumper into the bay," said Joe.

"Not quite that," Patrick said. "I got a call this morning from a friend of mine who owns the Family Arcade on Tenth Street and the Boardwalk in Ocean City. Today he was worried for the safety of some of the young female teenagers and also concerned someone would steal money from his arcade."

Cici walked over to him sitting on the couch. "Here's a glass of wine," she said.

"Thanks. My friend, Buck, heard that two arcades in Rehoboth Beach were hit the week before by a lone male about forty years old. He wasn't caught, and Buck was worried that his arcade would be robbed next. Buck asked me if I would stand around looking inconspicuous in the arcade while scanning the area until he closed up. He was right. The intruder broke in after Buck locked up. I had stopped on the Boardwalk out in front of the arcade after he locked up to watch a school of dolphins swimming in the ocean. I started walking back to my car parked on the side street when I heard a bang in the back alley and saw trash cans toppling over behind the arcade. This idiot had broken into the arcade, caused damage to the machine inside, and withdrew $300 worth of quarters. I nabbed him and held him there until the police came. They think he was the suspect who stole from the two other arcades in Rehoboth Beach. It was a successful day all around."

"Good job," said Crabbe. "And it was a good thing you stopped to watch the dolphins."

"So glad you caught him. Cici, can I help you in the kitchen?" asked Amie.

"No, almost done," said Cici.

"Where's Old Bay?" said Amie.

"Oh, that reminds me. I have to feed him. He doesn't like walking on the hardwood floors. He's happy lying on the carpet in our bedroom. His arthritis is getting worse."

"I'll feed him, Cici. You have to keep an eye on dinner," said Joe.

Cici got busy setting the table and lighting the candles with help from Amie. She called everyone to come to the table. They dined on fried eggplant topped with backfin lump crabmeat on the screened-in porch outside.

"It's delicious," said Amie.

Patrick grabbed his plate and headed back into the kitchen. "I'm having seconds."

"I think Lindsay wants some," said Cici.

"Who's Lindsay?" asked Amie.

Cici patted her tummy. "My baby girl."

"I thought you were naming her Rayne," said Amie.

"No, Joe and I are naming her after his mom. Lindsay Alison Crabbe," said Cici.

"That's a beautiful name," Amie said.

By the time they called it a night, it was 11:30 p.m. Amie left some of the dump cake that she had donated for dessert to Cici and Joe. "I just have to keep one slice of it for Patrick."

That night, before turning out their bedroom light, Patrick told Amie he was going to drive to Salisbury on Monday, August 31, to check on a few things before heading to work.

CHAPTER 12

On that same mild Saturday morning of the farmers market on August 29, Paul was up and about, brushing his teeth and listening to the "Delmarva Life" news on TV. He decided to go to the farmers market in Ocean Pines and buy some freshly baked goods and fruit. He drove his truck to the park and luckily pulled into a spot just as someone was leaving. Paul stopped at a booth and bought some tea towels and pot holders, which he needed for his new house. He then browsed in the many booths until he found the one he wanted. He purchased peach buns and a baguette baked just that morning. As the salesgirl was putting the items in a brown paper bag, Paul saw Amie across the way buying produce. He noticed she was with a pregnant lady. *Man, she looks familiar. Where have I seen that woman before?* Amie looked straight at him and then quickly turned her head to speak to the person behind the counter. Paul bolted around the corner and stayed behind a tree. He peeked out after a few minutes, and she was gone. He hoped she hadn't seen him. He could get into a lot of trouble for violating his probation agreement if Amie thought he was stalking her. *Would they believe I saw her by accident if she reported seeing me?*

Paul was dying to get another glimpse of her. She looked dazzling with her dark tan against her white, strapless summer dress and shiny flaxen hair. Paul walked around to the spot where she had last stood. He looked down the walkway surrounded by booths and glimpsed her outline at the far end of the aisle, strolling with her lady friend. He carefully followed her until they reached their car. Paul watched them load their packages into the back of a yellow convertible. Amie slid into the driver's seat and started the engine. *Looks like Amie got herself a nice, new little car.*

When Paul drove back to his apartment, he decided to assess his new house's needs. He wanted to buy carpeting for the four rooms and tile the cement floor on the screened-in porch. He felt self-adhesive vinyl floor planks would do the trick. He thought two comfortable chairs would be fine for the time being in the 12' x 15' living room. He remembered seeing a faux leather club chair as well as a caravan rattan papasan chair in the consignment shop that could work well in the living room. The leather had a rip in the back, but he could put the chair against the wall, and it wouldn't be noticeable. He'd use an end table from his apartment and put it between the two chairs and bring his TV folding tray to the small house. He didn't know if he'd pack up his flat-screen. Maybe the durable kitchen table would work nicely in the living room for his laptop. He'd watch what he wanted on Netflix on his iPad and forget the TV.

There were no closets in either of the bedrooms, so he thought he'd purchase a portable closet wardrobe organizer or maybe a double-rail clothes rack. In the interim, he'd live out of his suitcase with a minimal amount of clothes. He'd have to go to Mr. Bubbles Laundromat in Ocean City to wash his soiled clothes, because there was no washer or dryer in the small house. Luckily, his double bed would fit well into the bedroom. He needed furniture for the 14' x 11' porch, and he knew he could find a suitable outdoor set at the consignment shop. Paul had packed kitchen items, such as dishes, cups, bowls, glasses, and utensils from his apartment, and kept them in one cardboard box in his Ford pickup truck. He thought he'd replace the toilet and bathroom sink. Maybe call Bath Fitters.

Another purchase Paul decided on was a boat. He planned to take a look at various boats at the North Bay Marina in Selbyville, Delaware. He had his heart set on a twenty-four-foot Hurricane SunDeck, but it cost more than he cared to pay. He'd look at used boats too. Paul was pleased when he learned that he could dock a boat near the River Run Golf Course for a minimal cost.

He didn't know what to do with the decrepit shed and shanty on his property, but there was plenty of time to decide what to do about that.

Paul left at 4:00 p.m. on his last day of work, August 31, and drove his truck to Pittsville Ford on Old Ocean City Road. He asked the salesman there what the truck was worth. He wasn't ready to get rid of it yet, because he'd need it for his move to the new house. He then drove the truck to Ocean Lodge in Ocean City and spoke to the manager about staying there until the settlement date on his house. He wanted to rent a simple one-bedroom and bathroom and asked the manager what kind of deal he could give him while waiting until September 21. The manager quoted him $950, and Paul finagled him down to $825. He persuaded the manager that he would be renting it in the off season, and it should be less expensive because of that. *Much cheaper than paying another month's rent in the apartment.*

At 6:15 p.m., Paul met Matt and Tim to catch up on the latest. Kim was there too, sitting next to Tim. She was wearing a black-and-white bandeau dress that wrapped around her breasts. On her feet were pearl sandals. They chose to eat dinner at Waterman's on Route 50, because they could eat all the steamed crabs, corn, and shrimp they wanted. The wait wasn't too long before they walked up the steps, and the waitress showed them to a table for four.

Matt said. "I turned in the company car last week and bought a new Hyundai Santa Fe. We also sold our house."

"That was quick," said Tim.

"Yeah, a prof from Salisbury University and his wife bought it," said Matt. "But the best news is that I got the sales rep job."

"Good news," said Tim. "When are you actually moving?"

"I start training October 1, so we'll probably move to Baltimore before that," said Matt. "We'll stay with my in-laws until we find a house we like."

"I'm happy for you, buddy," said Paul. "Congratulations."

"I took the job at the gym," said Tim. "I'm still looking for that better-paying job, though."

Paul said, "Me too." He turned to look at Matt. "Listen, Matt. I have a proposition for you. Is Sally going to keep her Honda Accord? You've just bought a new Hyundai, and I'm going to need a new car too. Would she consider selling her Accord to me? I'll pay you above the Kelley Blue Book value. How about two thousand above? Isn't it a 2013 LX?"

"Yeah. I'll ask her. She might like a new car. I'll let you know," said Matt.

The crabs arrived steaming hot. Not much conversation flowed at the table. The food was too damn good to waste time on chatter. After dinner, Paul headed to the restroom. After he washed his hands and unlocked the door, Kim blocked his exit and walked inside. She turned around to lock the door. Startled, he couldn't hide his surprise, and his eyes widened and his lips slightly parted.

"I'm so sorry that you got laid off, Paul. I've always thought you were a hard worker and achiever. I admire that," she said as she put her hand on his shoulder. "Actually, Paul, I've always admired you." Paul's eyes brightened. He smiled and felt a twinge in his pants. "Paul, I've always been attracted to you."

Kim was good at being playful and saying the right things to men. Paul felt ambushed, but it was intoxicating. He felt her thick, curly brown hair on his cheek, and her perfumed fragrance excited him. She moved to kiss him hard on his lips. She brushed her body against his and grabbed his bulge between his legs. He unzipped his pants. "Nice," she said when she pulled his pants down. Paul hiked up her dress. They kissed again until Paul couldn't catch his breath. He was insanely turned on. They collapsed against the bathroom wall. Paul pinned her against the wall and drove himself inside her while she wrapped her legs around his hips. She gave Paul a huge rush, and when they were done, she lavished on him the most mischievous smile and caress. Paul gave her a huge grin back. "Don't tell Tim," she said, and she walked back out the door. Paul stood there smirking and zipped up his pants.

Tim and his working girl. She's definitely not Amie. Kim never could replace her.

Monday, August 31, that same day, Patrick headed to Salisbury. He pulled his Seville into the parking lot of Paul's apartment and didn't see Paul's Durango parked there. He then drove to Implant Products and spotted Paul's car in the rear parking lot behind the building. *Guess he's inside. I'll give Chip Hammond a call.*

"Chip Hammond," he said.

"Mr. Hammond, this is Patrick McCombe, private investigator."

"Yes, how are you Mr. McCombe?"

"Doing well, thanks," said Patrick. "I'm calling you about Paul Simmons. May I ask you a few questions?"

"Sure. I hope everything is OK," said Chip.

"So far, so good, thanks. Has Mr. Simmons been keeping his appointments with you?"

"Yes, he has. He's never canceled. We've met at his apartment three times now, and our next appointment is on September 8. In fact, Paul called me to set the date. He has a good attitude about making efforts to improve his problem with controlling his anger. Paul is attempting to follow the strategies we have thumbed through in several handouts. I know it's early, but I'm pleased with his willingness to change his ways."

"That sounds good. I hope you're right. Please let me know if there are any setbacks," said Patrick.

"Absolutely, Mr. McCombe, and the same goes for you."

Patrick felt relieved as he drove home.

That night he shared the information with Amie.

"Didn't you tell him I thought I saw him the other day?"

"No, Amie. I didn't. Are you totally sure you saw Paul at the farmers market?"

"Not completely sure, but I think it was him," Amie said.

"It's not enough to mention it, Amie," said Patrick.

"If it was Paul, I bet I encounter him again. I just feel I will. It's really distressing, Patrick. I'm constantly watching out for him…I just wish the judge had done more than he did. Throwing him in jail would have made me happy. I have this creepy feeing that Paul could be playing cat-and-mouse games with me right now," she said.

-🙢-

Paul filed for unemployment on September 3. That same day, he drove his truck back to his apartment parking lot, where he met Matt and Sally because she had agreed to sell him her Honda Accord. He wanted them to think he still lived in an apartment there.

Paul paid her $17,000 in cash for the Honda. They signed the title over to Paul and gave him a receipt for the cash.

"I'll return the tags and license plate to save you guys the hassle," said Paul. But he wasn't really planning on returning them. He glanced at the license plate and saw that the registration didn't need to be renewed for another two years. Now, he wouldn't have to buy a car that would have to be registered at the Department of Motor Vehicles. He could just keep the license plate on the Honda and sell it in two years when the registration had to be renewed. He hoped that by not registering the Honda, it would be more difficult to find him. At least it would be more problematic for Patrick.

On September 8, Paul met Chip at his office on the third floor in one of the state office buildings in Salisbury. "Hey, how's it going?" asked Chip.

"Very well, thanks," said Paul.

"You like it better here than meeting at your apartment?" asked Chip.

"Yes," said Paul.

"Why didn't you want to keep meeting at your apartment?" asked Chip.

"Honestly, Chip, I don't want any of my close friends to find out I'm on probation. It's embarrassing. I had to lie last time that you were my neighbor when one of my coworkers stopped by. I didn't like lying, but it's my personal business, and I didn't want it to get around at work. I hope you understand. Plus, your office is closer to my workplace than the apartment," said Paul.

"Of course, I understand," said Chip. "I did overhear what your coworker was saying. Something about rumors going around at your workplace. Everything OK at Implants?"

"Yeah," Paul snorted. *Nosy guy.* "The VP of sales got caught looking at porn more than once on his computer at work. The guys were just talking about what would happen if he were fired. Two of us might be interested in his position if he was let go, but he's still there. We haven't heard anything about his being fired yet," said Paul.

"Are you one of the two guys interested in his position?" asked Chip.

"I was thinking about it, but it looks like the VP is staying."

"Well, good luck with that," said Chip. "Now, how about we go over anger management strategies from the handout I gave you. Did you keep a log like I asked?"

"Yes, I did. I wrote down two instances that happened. One was when I got angry at this guy who cut me off driving to work. I slammed the palm of my hand on the horn and wanted to scream obscenities out the car window at him. Then I took several deep breaths and decided that it wouldn't do any good, because he wouldn't hear me anyway with his window up. The second incident was when I was shopping in Food Lion, and they were out of my brand of ice tea. At first, I wanted to march over to the manager and give him a piece of my mind, but again, I practiced inhaling, holding my breath, and exhaling four times. So I chose another brand of ice tea, and…" He laughed. "It's actually better tasting than the one I drink all the time." *You gullible moron.*

"That's progress, Paul. You're learning to cope better. Good job. Name other ways you can control your anger," Chip said.

Paul recited some of the strategies to Chip that he remembered from the brochure. *This is so stupid. Do I get a sticker? What am I, in second grade? This has got to stop.*

"Continue to keep your log, and try to use some of the strategies you just told me from the brochure next time," said Chip. They ended their meeting twenty minutes later, and Paul told Chip he'd call him to set next month's date.

I need to be in control. I hate these meetings.

Paul ended up buying a used twenty-two-foot 2011 SunDeck Sport Hurricane boat that suited his budget much better. The previous owner had kept it in excellent condition, and the 150 Yamaha engine was only one year old. He went out for a spin on the boat with the owner of the marina on Assawoman Bay. Out on the water, the tide opposed a stiff breeze, and things got dicey. It was a bit bumpy as they cruised twelve knots in the bay. But Paul loved the bouncing and the spray smacking his face. As he slowed down a bit, he found the steering was smooth, and the radio worked. This would be fun.

He kept the boat at a pier near River Run Golf Course, not too far from his small house. The wharf's planks were old and rickety, and Paul had to look down and watch every step he took walking along the pier to a path that led to the River Run Golf Club. Such a beautiful golf course, but such an unstable, ugly pier. A few boards had been replaced, but others were tilted and cracked. If he wasn't careful, his leg could go right through one of the rotten wooden slats. He hopped over many of the planks that looked like they would fall into the river if you stepped down too hard on them. But the inexpensive monthly fee to dock his boat there was worth it.

CHAPTER 13

On September 18, Amie lugged her carrying case to the parking lot. It was loaded with contracts and listings of new and old houses in the Delmarva area. *This car is wicked cool! I love it!* She got into her Mini Cooper, put the case in the back seat, remotely put her convertible top down, and zoomed toward home. Amie didn't get very far, as the car was wobbling along Racetrack Road. She managed to pull onto the side of the road. *Now what?*

Paul just happened to drive by and swung over to the right side of the road. He got out of his truck and walked over to Amie's Mini Cooper. "Looks like your front right tire is flat."

Amie looked up at him and wanted to yell to passersby, but she thought better of it. She was stuck there on a busy, heavily traveled highway and decided to stay put. "Oh, is that what's wrong?"

"Do you have a spare in the trunk?" asked Paul.

She popped the trunk open, and Paul hoisted the spare tire out of her trunk and set to work changing her tire. While she sat behind the steering wheel, she took her lipstick mace spray out of her purse and put it on her lap. Amie's cell phone buzzed, and Cici was on the other end. Feeling her heart pumping inside her chest, Amie told Cici what was happening. Cici kept her on the line until Paul finished changing the tire. He put the damaged tire into the back of his truck along with his jack. He walked over to her car. "All done; you're as good as new. You look fabulous."

Amie started the engine. "Thanks. I really appreciate it." Paul slammed her trunk door shut. "I'd better go," she yelled back to him, and off she went like a bullet.

That bastard did it. I bet he punctured my tire. He did it while I was in the realtor's office. But how did he know what kind of car I drive? I'm not going to file a report with the police on this. The creep did change my tire.

And that night, Amie entered the incident into her log, not forgetting the date and time.

And that night Patrick checked the tire on Amie's car but didn't see the damaged tire. He searched for a GPS tracker that Paul might have installed under her Mini Cooper.

And that night, Paul hugged Amie's bra and panties to his chest.

Settlement on September 21 went smoothly. Paul had checked out of Ocean Lodge in the morning before heading to the title company. It was a humid day for the move, nearly reaching eighty-nine degrees. He enlisted the services of a consignment store to drop off the chairs and an outdoor set for his new house later that afternoon. Paul had consigned most of the apartment furniture that he couldn't use anywhere in the little house. Without help, he stacked two boxes, his double bed, mattress, box spring, two end tables, and a TV folding tray, and loaded them all into his Ford truck. Unpacking was an unpleasant task, given the heat outside and also because he had little storage to house items. He left the second bedroom empty, and he stored one box under his bed. From the other box, he emptied notions and various miscellaneous items, such as detergent, paper plates and cups, plastic utensils, a few tools, a couple of pairs of shoes, and dry goods. The moving truck from the consignment shop arrived with his two chairs and porch furniture around 4:00 p.m. Paul was famished after the work he did that day. The maid came shortly after that and spent an hour cleaning. After Paul paid and tipped the maid, he drove his Honda to Light House Sound's Golf Club and ordered light fare in their bar. Gazing out the clubhouse windows at the Saint Martin's River, he relaxed, sipping his ice-cold draft beer and finishing his medium-rare hamburger.

He slept fairly well the first two weeks in his new surroundings. It took several nights to get used to the loud humming and clicking of the cicadas. Screeches, chirps, and the yapping of foxes woke Paul up in the middle of the night at times, but after a while, the strange nocturnal sounds in the woods delighted him. He even took some extra patience to identify the individual calls. Eventually, Paul grew to live in harmony with the noises. *Beats car honks and blaring fire trucks any day.*

He thought it best to purchase a .22-caliber gun for protection. Paul wasn't a fan of guns. His mother never would allow his father to have one in the house, but living on the outskirts surrounded by woodlands, Paul felt safer having one. He wasn't sure where to hide it in the house and decided to conceal it in the glove compartment of his Honda when the opportunity arose.

He sold his Ford truck in Pittsville, and one of the workers at the dealership kindly dropped him off at his old apartment so he could pick up the Honda, which he left there the day he bought it from Sally. He then drove the Honda to the Ocean Pines post office. He wasn't expecting any mail and found the box crammed only with junk mail. That evening, he sat in his comfy living room chair and watched season four of *Breaking Bad* on Netflix while eating a Stouffer's country fried pork chop. *Love that man Walter White.*

September 30, Amie showered in the locker room and dressed in her legwarmers and a tank top after working out in the Ocean Pines Fitness Center. She had been a member there for six years. As she was leaving, she glanced to her left and saw Paul rise and strain from lifting weights in a glass-enclosed room. She confirmed with the lady at the entrance desk that Paul had recently joined her fitness club.

Are you kidding me? I can't shrug this off. Amie checked on him again. She made sure he was looking forward, viewing himself as he hefted his weights in the lengthy metallic mirror opposite him. *Hope he didn't see my reflection. And hope the barbell falls on his toes.*

When Amie arrived home, she checked her emails and saw one from Paul. "Patrick, come in here."

"What's wrong?" he asked.

"Look at this." Patrick sat beside her at their large L-shaped storage desk. He leaned forward to read Paul's email on Amie's cell phone.

> Amie, let's get back together. I expected more appreciation from you when I changed your

tire. Why do you treat me like I'm dirt? We were so good together. The guy you're married to is useless. You deserve so much better than that. I'm beginning to think you are really foolish. My mother loved you. She always talked about us getting married. She said we were perfect for each other. Please give me another chance. I can make you happy. Not him. He's second rate. Forevermore I will wait for you. Call me. We have to talk.

"Son of a bitch. Where are you going?" asked Patrick.

"Let's see if he left me any voice mails on our phone," said Amie as she walked into the kitchen to check the landline. "Yep. There's a voice mail from Paul." Patrick and she listened to it together.

"Listen, bitch. I'm getting a little pissed off you haven't called me. I sent you email about us getting back together. I know you're married. Have you heard about this thing called divorce? You're really letting me down, Amie. I can't stand a woman who doesn't realize what's good for her. You disappoint me. Your husband is a lowlife. Sometimes I think about giving you a good spanking over my knee. What's it going to take for you to understand you shouldn't be with that jerk of a man that you married? You have a distorted view of life. Being with that man is sickening. Wake up. You're an intelligent woman, but I need to teach you how to be smarter. I could just kill you; you make me so mad."

"This is a threatening message. He's broken his probation agreement. He broke it when he changed your tire, but you let it go. I'm positive we'll get a restraining order now. I'll apply for it as soon as possible. I want to see his ass in jail. Amie, I don't mean to frighten you, but he's crossed the line, and I'm afraid he could try to harm you," said Patrick.

"Or kill me? You think he could do that?" Amie asked.

"I don't trust him, Amie. He could do anything…even that," said Paul. "He's one sick bastard."

Patrick notified Chip Hammond of the voice mail and the tire incident.

⚐

Two hours later, Paul saw Chip's number appear on his iPhone. He answered. "Hi, Chip. What's up?"

"I know this is short notice, but I wondered if you would be able to meet tomorrow for our next meeting," said Chip. "I just found out I have to go to a seminar for two weeks, and I'm really busy after that. I want to be sure I can fit you in for our October appointment."

"Tomorrow works for me," said Paul.

"Do you still want to meet at my office?"

"Yes, I prefer your office, if you don't mind," said Paul.

"Just want to make sure. I forgot to ask you the two questions last time that I'm supposed to ask each time we meet. Are you still living at Shady Pines Apartments?"

"Yes."

"And are you still working at Implant Products?"

"Yes."

"OK, I'll see you tomorrow at 5:15 p.m."

"Perfect."

⚐

The next day, on October 1, Chip, Patrick, and a security guard sat in Chip's office at the Parole and Probation Offices on Baptist Street in the Multi-Service Center in Salisbury. Patrick wore khaki pants, an oxford blue shirt, and a navy-blue jacket. He was overdressed compared to Chip in his sport shirt and jeans.

Chip looked at his watch. It was almost 5:30 p.m. Patrick looked out Chip's office window, which overlooked the parking lot. Patrick didn't see Paul's Dodge Durango anywhere. "Has he ever been late before?" asked Patrick.

"No, he's always been on time," said Chip. He dialed Paul's number and heard, "The number is unavailable at the moment."

At 6:00 p.m. Paul hadn't arrived at Chip's office. It was obvious Paul hadn't planned to show up. Chip told Patrick that violating probation is a crime in itself, and the consequences could be serious, but Patrick already knew that. It was more serious now because Paul had left Amie a threatening voice mail message.

CHAPTER 14

Amie jumped when she heard the back kitchen door bang shut. Patrick entered and threw a portfolio on top of the kitchen table.

"You scared me to death!" said Amie. "Why didn't you call me and give me a heads-up that you were coming home early?"

"I'm sorry, babe," said Patrick.

"You should be," she said, raising her voice.

"Amie, you've had a short fuse these past days."

"Well, what do you expect? You said Paul could kill me. I'm a nervous wreck," she said, folding her arms across her chest. "Suppose one of your exes was stalking you? Like in the movie *Fatal Attraction?* You'd be on edge," Amie said.

"You're right. How could I forget that? His mistress stalked him and drove him crazy. She boiled a bunny in a pot in their house."

"Yep," said Amie, crossing her arms.

"Amie, I'm sorry. I love you so much, and I don't want anything bad happening to you. I'm going to find him." Patrick wrapped his arms around her to comfort her. He kissed her forehead. "I filed for a restraining order. We have good cause this time."

"What good will that do? He'll try to kill me no matter what," said Amie.

⊨

The next morning, Amie made an appointment with her primary care physician, Dr. Henderson, whom she guessed had to be in his midsixties. He reminded her of John McCain. She felt so sheltered in his presence. He listened to Amie with a sympathetic ear. Like a beloved grandfather. She told Dr. Henderson every detail of what she had experienced the last five months with Paul. "I can't sleep," she said. "I'm too uneasy showing a house to a male stranger. I need to have someone accompany me. I'm nervous when I go to work. Can you give me something to calm me down?"

"Amie, I normally prescribe Xanax or Ativan for patients who have a history of anxiety disorder or panic attacks. I wouldn't want you to have a dependency on these types of drugs. You could become addicted to the point where you couldn't curb your anxiety without these substances. Are you unable to concentrate?"

"No, I'm able to," said Amie.

"Are you irritable?"

"Yes, with Patrick at times, but not at work."

"Do you have difficulty breathing?"

"No."

"Do you feel depressed?"

"Not really."

"In my opinion, you don't have an anxiety disorder and certainly no history of that or of panic attacks. But anxiety is a normal physiological reaction to certain stressful situations. There are other ways to help you relax, such as a therapeutic massage. I would recommend you try other means to get through this difficult time. I'm so sorry you're experiencing this. But I can suggest a therapist or a psychiatrist you could see if this anxiousness becomes excessive."

"Thank you," said Amie. "I'll think about it. I just hope they catch him soon."

⚓

October 2, Patrick drove to Salisbury to the Shady Pines Apartments. He was on a hunt. Since Patrick hadn't seen Paul's Durango in the parking lot outside Chip's office that day, Patrick asked Amie if she noticed if Paul had been driving his black truck the day he changed her tire. That day, Amie couldn't really see anything out of her rearview mirror because the open trunk lid was obscuring her view as she sat in the driver's seat. Her mind wasn't occupied with noticing what kind of car Paul was driving. She was itching to get away from him as soon as possible after he finished changing the tire.

Patrick saw no Durango in Paul's apartment's parking lot. Nor was there a black truck. He knocked on the landlord's ajar office door and walked into his office.

"Hi, I'm Detective Patrick McCombe." He flipped open his wallet to show his ID. "I'm looking for Paul Simmons. He has violated his probation, and we're trying to find him. Are you the landlord?"

"I'm the manager of these apartments, but I can tell you he doesn't live here anymore."

"Do you have any idea where he went?"

"No sir. Sorry," said the manager.

Patrick had had a feeling he wouldn't be there. He drove over to Implant Products and found the sales manager after identifying himself to the receptionist. "I'm looking for Paul Simmons, who works here," said Patrick.

"He doesn't work here anymore," said the sales manager.

Patrick's brow wrinkled. "What? Where does he work now?"

"Sorry, I don't know. He got laid off with a number of people on August 31."

Patrick said, "I saw his Dodge Durango in the parking lot. I guess they're company cars?"

"Yes, from the old company," said the manager. "The laid-off employees had to turn their company cars in."

"The old company?" asked Patrick.

"Yes. We are Ortho-Designs. Implant Products was bought out. We're waiting for the new sign to be switched out in the front of the building yet."

Patrick headed back to his Bishopville office. *Paul's one sneaky, slimy snake.* He gathered his associates around him in his office. "We need to find Paul Simmons. He's left his apartment, was laid off from his job, and had to turn in his company car. Let's check other apartments, hotels, and motels in Salisbury, Ocean City, and Ocean Pines. Find out if any houses in Ocean Pines and Ocean City sold recently." *Amie could probably help us with that.*

"Simmons was looking at houses in Ocean Pines to buy. Also look at recently sold houses or condos in Salisbury. Joe, I'll need a DMV check to see what car he's driving now. Also, we need to find out if he still has his Ford F-150."

"What's going on?" Patrick's receptionist asked.

"I'm concerned for the safety of my wife. Everyone, Simmons violated his probation agreement and didn't show up for his last meeting with his officer." He explained to his coworkers about the last voice mail Paul had sent to Amie. "We have to work fast. He's capable of doing anything now."

Two days later, Patrick got a hit. Joe Crabbe said, "He stayed at the Ocean Lodge in Ocean City from September 1 until September 21."

Patrick hopped in his SUV and drove over the Route 90 Bridge to the Ocean Lodge. Patrick walked under the blinking Vacancy sign and stepped inside the main office. He identified himself to the woman behind the reception desk.

"Can you tell me when Paul Simmons left your facility?"

The elderly gray-haired lady typed on the monitor, looked at the computer, and said, "September 21."

"Do you know why he left?" asked Patrick.

"No. Sorry."

"Is there a landlord or manager around here?"

"Yes, but he won't be back until tomorrow. He's out of town."

Patrick thanked her and told her he'd be back the next day.

The next morning when Patrick returned to his office, Joe told him that the DMV had come up empty. "He did sell his truck to Pittsville Ford, though. I called them, and they told me they paid him cash for the truck but couldn't give me any more information than that."

"Another dead end," said Patrick. "But good work, though. Little by little we'll find him. I have to drive back to Ocean Lodge."

At Ocean Lodge, Patrick parked his car under the Vacancy sign out front. He found the manager. "I understand Paul Simmons rented a room from you but checked out September 21. Do you know where he went, by any chance?"

"No, sorry," the husky manager said.

Paul sighed. "There's a warrant out for his arrest."

The manager asked, "Really? What did he do?"

Patrick told him about the violation.

"Did he say anything else about why he was leaving?"

The manager said, "He only mentioned that he had a settlement on a house on the day he left."

"That's a big help. Thanks," said Patrick, and he dashed out of the office.

Patrick's team checked all the title companies in Ocean City and Salisbury that had settlements on September 21. Patrick learned that Paul settled September 21 at Capitol Real Estate Title Company on Coastal Highway in Ocean City, Maryland.

CHAPTER 15

Paul figured McCombe or the police would try to find him for not keeping his appointment with his probation officer. He knew that once they traced his address, they'd locate him, and he would have to go back to court. Paul didn't want to be caught. He didn't want them to find him in his house, so he decided to stay away from it for a while. He figured out ways he could remain concealed from the police and Detective McCombe.

First, he parked his charcoal-colored Honda Accord at River Run's Golf Course parking lot, in the back near the residential area. He walked back to his house, which was about a mile away. Second, he tidied up the place and took the settlement contract, photos, and other personal papers and slipped them inside his backpack. He then stripped the bed. He staged the interior of the house to look as barren as possible.

Don't want it to appear that I'm actually living here.

Third, he packed clothes, checkbooks, cell phone, cash, flashlight, pocketknife, and snacks in his backpack. In addition to his backpack, he planned to carry a sleeping bag and take his laptop with him. Fourth, he kept his front door unlocked because if the police found out where he lived, he didn't want them to kick in his door. Fifth, he headed to his boat docked at the neglected mini marina near the golf course.

The path to the L-shaped pier was covered in pine cones, pebbles, twigs, and several dirty golf balls from the driving range. His boat was docked at the far end of the pier. He scrambled down the dirt path to the boat, twigs snapping and leaves crunching beneath his sneakers.

Paul started the engine of his boat and cruised down the Saint Martin's River, finally docking at Harpoon Hannah's for a bite to eat. He ate bacon-wrapped scallops, boom-boom shrimp, and crabby waffle fries. Paul drank a Captain's Mai Tai and took a slice of coconut cake to go.

The sun set while Paul's boat thrashed through the river. After passing under the bridge, he decelerated and eventually found a remote spot in a secluded cove, away from any houses. He coasted closer to land and anchored there. When it was completely dark, he crawled inside his sleeping bag on the floor near the stern and nodded off.

The next morning, the bright sun jolted him out of a sound sleep. It was eerily quiet and beautiful in the cove. He watched a blue heron stretch out its long neck and wings at the water's edge. Maybe it was wading and searching for prey. *Speaking of prey, I'm hungry.* Paul opened his cardboard box and ate the coconut cake and an apple from his backpack for breakfast. *Lucky for me, it's a nice day, around sixty-five degrees and not raining. Think I'll cruise by Amie's house on the Assawoman Bay.*

Paul didn't make it to cruise by Amie's house in his boat. Dark clouds drifted in, and he didn't want to chance getting caught in a storm. He headed back to the pier and docked his boat. He left his sleeping bag under one seat and snapped the canvas cover over it. Paul slipped his arms through his backpack straps and walked back to his car in the golf course lot. He drove to the post office to check if he had any mail in his PO box. It was empty except for his first severance paycheck.

Raindrops covered Paul's windshield. He turned on his wipers. The Wave on 97.1 FM reported that there would be heavy showers in the Delmarva area. Paul didn't want to risk returning to his house. He drove to McDonald's on Racetrack Road, washed his face and hands in the restroom, and ordered lunch. He ate his Deluxe Quarter Pounder in his car after he parked it at the side of the building. Paul then cashed his severance check at his bank's drive-through and put the money in his backpack. He called the Fenwick Marina. He made an appointment for them to haul away his boat, shrink wrap it for the upcoming winter season, and keep it at their facility. He had to figure out what to do next.

After reaching Tim on his cell phone, he headed to Salisbury.

⚔

Tuesday, October 6, Patrick and Hulk met with the closing agent at Capitol Real Estate Title Company in Ocean City, Maryland, late in the afternoon. The closing agent had an animated face and flashed her teeth in a wide smile. She was a large woman, but Hulk still dwarfed her size when he stood next to her. "Pleased to meet you," she said. "I'm Leslie O'Connor. Now, what specifically can I do to help you?" she asked as she brushed strands of chestnut hair away from her face.

"Glad to meet you," said Patrick. "Chief Phillips and I need to find a man named Paul Simmons. He violated his probation and is not living at his previous address any longer. We understand that he settled on a property at your title company on September 21."

Hulk said, "We need his address, ma'am."

Ms. O'Connor looked at the tall, beefy, overweight man. "Of course, I remember him." She sat down on her swivel chair, her broad hips protruding over the seat's edge. She faced the computer screen with her back to them. She stared at her monitor and typed in the necessary information. Retrieving what they needed, she said, "Here it is. Paul Simmons. He bought a home on a one-acre wooded lot in Berlin, Maryland. The address is 592 Windmill Creek Road."

"Hulk, do you know where that is?" asked Patrick.

"I have no idea," said Hulk.

Ms. O'Connor said, "Here's a map of the property. I can print it off for you."

Hulk and Patrick thanked her and left her office with the printed copy of the map. "Let's hope he's home," said Hulk.

Finding the property was fairly easy. Patrick sat next to Hulk in his car. It bumped and jerked along the dirt-covered driveway to a clearing. "Sure is a long, narrow road," said Hulk. "Is that his house? It's a rattrap," said Hulk. He laughed out loud. "Are you kidding me? I thought he had money."

"Yeah, me too. Why in the hell would he buy this proper-ty...way in the woods, away from everything?" asked Patrick. "There's no sign of his car anywhere."

Hulk pulled his patrol car around the clearing and parked it at the edge of the circular dirt driveway. They walked up to the house, but in order to knock on the front door, they had to traipse through the screened-in porch. Hulk loudly rapped on the door. "Mr. Simmons, this is Chief Phillips. Open the door, please."

They heard no response from inside and decided to enter the home. The door was unlocked. The musty air hit them in the face when they entered the living room. "Mr. Simmons?" said Hulk as he coughed.

They searched the small house. "You think he lives here? There's just a mattress on the bed. No toothbrush or stuff is in the medicine cabinet," said Hulk. "Just a small towel and a bar of soap."

"There's little in the fridge except for some milk, cheese, and catsup," said Patrick.

"Ooh, the milk's sour," Hulk said, sniffing the bottle and making a face. "There are no dishes or glasses."

"Doesn't look like he's completely moved in yet. There's a film of dust on top of this table." With his index finger, he drew a line in the dust.

"Well, I'll just have to wait for his arrival every night," said Patrick. He told Hulk to go home and that he was going to stay the night at Paul's house. "I'll call you in the morning to pick me up. I'm going to tell Amie to spend the night at Cici and Joe's house."

"Think you're gonna catch this dude?" Hulk asked. "He could have gone out of town."

"I'm going to catch him, Hulk."

Paul met Tim at their favorite spot for a beer. They chatted awhile, and Tim told Paul that he was still looking for a job. "Maybe I should move to Baltimore like Matt and Sally," said Tim. "This job at the gym is boring, and it's so little pay for the long hours. How about you?"

"No luck so far. I was thinking maybe of getting a job in Ocean City at a hotel as a waiter."

"Oh, that's not for me," said Tim. "Say, how do you like Sally's Honda?"

"I like it a lot," said Paul. "Are you living with Kim?"

"No, I need my freedom. Don't want to start that," Tim said. "I'm going to keep renting my two-bedroom condo."

They talked some more, played darts, and watched golf on the big-screen TV in the bar, and then Paul finally called it a day and drove back to Ocean Pines. Paul remembered the houses for sale nestled in the woods that he looked at back in May in Ocean Pines near Amie's house. He recalled one on Boston Road that backed up to Manklin Creek. The house had been on the market and had been vacant for almost a year when he had last seen it. It had been in great need of updating inside and would require a new roof. It was hard to see the neighboring houses on either side of the vacant house because of the thick pines bordering each lot.

Paul decided to drive by it again. He slowly accelerated by the house and saw that it was still for sale. It did not appear that the houses on either side of the empty house were occupied. October was a quiet time in Ocean Pines. Summer was over. People had left their beach houses to go home. Boston Road felt abandoned without people walking their dogs and without kids riding their bikes up and down the street. Paul decided to drive back later that night when it was dark to check out the area one more time. He drove to the Ocean Pines Library, settled in a chair in the rear of the room, and looked at magazines. After closing, Paul left the library and grabbed some fried chicken from Royal Farm for his late dinner.

Around 10:00 p.m., Paul drove back to the vacant house and was satisfied that Boston Road seemed deserted. He parked his Honda four houses down on the other side of the street in front of an empty lot. He sneaked back to the Boston Road house, shining his flashlight as he walked around to the back of the house which faced the creek. He neatly made a long slit in the porch screen with his pocketknife. He pushed the screen inward and stepped through the space. Paul bedded down on the outdoor three-seat wicker cushioned sofa, laying his head on a soft blue pillow, and fell asleep thinking of Amie. At 3:00 a.m., he woke up to the sound of thunder and rain. It poured for hours. The lightning kept him awake. What a miserable night on the porch.

The next morning, October 7, the sun reflected glowingly on Manklin Creek's water. Paul felt drowsy but wanted to leave the soaking-wet porch as soon as possible and headed to his car. He thought that another night sleeping on the boat, or on someone else's porch, or in his Honda Accord, was a bad idea. He drove to River Run's golf course, parked his Honda, and then showered in the men's locker room. He threw his slept-in T-shirt in the wastebasket and slipped on a fresh one out of his backpack. In the mirror he saw his stubble and stroked it with his thumb and forefinger. It would soon turn into a scruffy beard if he didn't shave. Paul figured he would go back to his house and check to see if it appeared that someone had been there while he had been gone. But first he'd have a crab melt sandwich at the Player's Club.

He left his Honda in the River Run Golf Course parking lot and strolled back to his house through the woods. When he was in a thicket at the rear of his house, he peered out to see if anyone's car was parked in the clearing. He saw no signs of life. Paul walked up to the front of his house, glanced down the driveway, and then entered his porch and front door. Nothing was disturbed. It looked as if the sparse house had had no visitors while he was gone. He trekked back to his car and decided he'd return to his house that night, take the risk, and spend a night or two in his own comfortable bed, no sheets and all. He checked to see if his flashlight was in his backpack and made sure he wouldn't forget it when he tramped through the woods to return to his house that night.

⊀

Patrick stayed the night sleeping in Paul's living room chair October 6 without nabbing him. But he didn't want to give up just yet. He called Hulk the morning of October 7 and asked him to pick him up at Paul's house at 7:30 a.m.

Hulk said, "I told you he's somewhere else," as Patrick slid into the car seat next to Hulk.

"I'm going to stay another night," Patrick said. "I'll have Joe drop me off tonight. You can take a break."

"OK, suit yourself. Good luck with staying there another night. I'd hate to spend the night in that ghastly place. Moldy old hut."

Patrick laughed. "That's right. I understand how you feel. He doesn't have a super jumbo king-size bed in there for you."

"Ha ha ha," said Hulk.

C HAPTER 16

Patrick was relaxing in Paul's rattan chair in the living room at 6:45 p.m. the night of October 7. The huge chair was actually quite comfortable. He rose from the comfy chair occasionally and then would step outside on the porch to listen for any cars coming up the driveway.

He familiarized himself again with the inside of the house. In case he had to pee in the middle of the night, he took note of the placement of the light switch that turned on the ceiling light fixture. Patrick was tired because he hadn't slept well the night before. He began playing Words with Friends on his iPhone but dozed off in the chair after the fourth game.

Three hours later, Patrick's eyes flew open. He thought he heard a noise outside. There it was again. *Squeak.* The screen door. Patrick immediately got up, put his iPhone in his pocket, and crept silently but quickly toward the front door. He heard footsteps coming closer. He pulled out his Glock .22 from his waistband and hid behind the door.

Paul walked in and switched on the light next to the front door.

"Stay right where you are, shithead," said Patrick.

Paul swerved around. Stunned, he gasped. His eyes widened.

"Raise your arms." Patrick paused. "All the way up." Patrick dialed Hulk's number and told him he had Paul Simmons at his house.

"I'll get backup," said Hulk.

Paul suddenly brought his arms down hard, striking Patrick's wrists and knocking the phone out of his left hand and causing the gun in his right hand to go off, firing a bullet into the carpet. Paul scrambled out of the house and ran toward the woods. Patrick picked up his gun and phone and chased him. It was pitch black, and he was guided only by the rustle of leaves and the crunching of fallen branches as Paul tore through the woods. Patrick wished he had a flashlight. It was way too dark. He would be lucky to catch him. He was glad he had called Hulk. Right now he would benefit from a search party.

As it turned out, Patrick wouldn't need a flashlight or search party because it wasn't long before he heard a piercing scream. It was coming from Paul. He shouted, "Back here. I'm back here. Help me. Hurry!"

"Keep yelling so I can get to you," said Patrick. The woods were so dark and thick that finding him was still challenging. Patrick turned and saw headlights in the distance back at Paul's house. *Must be Hulk.* He walked toward Paul's voice. "I'm coming. I'll be there soon." Patrick used his iPhone to inform Hulk to come into the woods and call 911.

"Hurry, please!" Paul yelled. Patrick finally reached him and saw Paul on the ground grabbing his ankle. Paul's injured right foot shone in the beam of his flashlight. "I've been bit by a snake. The flashlight was shining on it. It could have been a copperhead. It had hourglass- shaped crossbands and a bright-yellow tail tip. Take me to the hospital. God, it hurts. My foot's on fire, and it's rolling up to my knee. Put a tourniquet around my leg."

Hulk ran close to them. "I heard what you just said. No, don't do that. Leave him alone," Hulk said, wheezing and trying to catch his breath.

Backup arrived. All they could do now was wait for the ambulance.

⚚

Traveling in the ambulance was not pleasant for Paul. Every bump in the road made him wince. Curse words flew out of this mouth. "Shit, it hurts like hell."

Patrick was inside the ambulance with Paul. He ignored Paul's complaints and was glad the paramedic was tending to him. Patrick called Amie, undeterred by Paul's moaning.

"Amie, we caught Paul. I'm in the ambo with him heading to the hospital." He paused. "Because he was bitten by a snake. It's a long story." Pause. "Yes. I'm fine. Paul will be seeing a judge after he recuperates from his ordeal." He paused again. "Yeah, it's too late to go home, so stay the night at Cici's house. I'll see you in the morning. Hulk is meeting me at the hospital. Go to bed." Patrick hung up and knew Amie would sleep well for the first time in a long time.

Paul was rushed into the emergency room at Atlantic General Hospital in Berlin, where the nurses and a physician's assistant started an intravenous drip of normal saline and morphine. The nurse and the PA took a blood sample and hooked him up to the monitor. His blood pressure and temperature were taken, and his heart rate was monitored.

Outside Paul's exam room, Patrick heard him yell, "Stop pushing on my foot!" The young physician's assistant, Blair Hines, came out of Paul's cubicle. He had brown, curly hair and sizeable protruding ears. He stood next to Patrick.

"It sounds like he was bit by a copperhead. His description fits. Copperheads are not as deadly as other snakes. They do have venom, though, and are aggressive. What was he doing in the woods and marsh at this hour of the night?" Blair asked.

"He's a fugitive," said Paul. "Is the bite fatal?"

"The good news is that their venom is mild, and their bites are rarely ever fatal in humans. Copperheads are generally more aggressive at night. They rest in the daytime and are on the prowl at night for prey. But even cats and dogs often survive just fine, even without medication."

"Do you know how much venom he got from the snake?" asked Patrick.

"Not sure yet. A lethal dose is about a hundred milligrams. Sometimes the copperhead will give a warning bite first if it is stepped on, which releases very little venom or no venom at all."

"How do you know so much about copperheads?" asked Patrick.

"Oh, we get a few people who come in during the summer. We've treated golfers who have been bitten on courses in the tall grasses and water. It's usually because they look for their lost balls in the overgrown rough. Also, people who have gone hiking in the woods, who weren't very careful, have come in here with copperhead bites."

The attending physician, Dr. Lanning, came out of the ER to speak to Hulk and Patrick in the waiting area. He looked young, maybe thirty-five years old, and stared at them with large, heavy-lidded eyes framed with thick eyelashes and dark-black brows.

"He has two puncture wounds with a lot of swelling and redness around them. He has experienced difficulty breathing and complains of blurred vision. We are still assessing the bite wound. The plan now is to let him rest. This problem is managed by observation and rarely requires an antivenom. I'm going to go back inside and check on him," the doctor said.

Blair, the PA, said, "We have a scoring system we use and other indicators to see if he will need an antivenom or not. He'll be watched carefully for circulation, vital signs, and airway breathing. More signs could show up in the first couple of hours. They'll give him Benadryl and antibiotics."

Hulk turned to Patrick. "Why don't you go home? I'll keep you in the loop if anything changes. The doc knows Simmons committed a crime. I'll have a detective outside his cubicle tonight. Go get some sleep."

Patrick said, "Thanks, I will. How come you didn't want to put a tourniquet on him?"

"He could lose his leg if we had done that. With no blood flow, toxic waste can build up in his limb. Then when you release the tourniquet, all the toxic waste is going to flood the body. I should've let you put a tourniquet on him."

Patrick scoffed. "He's already a toxic waste," he said.

Patrick notified Joe Crabbe, giving him an update on Paul. Amie and Cici were sleeping soundly when he called.

Joe said, "Yeah, they'll no doubt have to keep him overnight. They don't like to give the antivenom because of the long-term effects on the liver and kidneys. Where did he get bit?"

Patrick said, "Inside the right heel. He screamed as soon as it happened."

"I guess so," said Joe.

"Good thing he yelled, because I don't think I would have found him in the dark. I'll see you tomorrow, and we'll find out what tomorrow brings for Simmons," said Patrick.

In the morning, Patrick, Hulk, and Joe learned that overnight, Paul experienced respiratory distress, low blood pressure, nosebleeds, and vomiting. And, of course, lots of pain. The doctor gave him the antivenom and explained it was a moderate dosage.

"Must have been a nasty snake," said Hulk. "Couldn't have happened to a nicer guy."

⚜

Paul spent time in the ICU after being treated with the antivenom. After that, he stayed in the hospital for two days. The nurse walked in to check his blood pressure. Paul said, "I'm so lethargic."

She said, "It's only normal right now to feel that way after what you've been through." She started to wash his body.

"My skin burns when you wash it."

"It'll stop doing that in a few days," the nurse said.

Chip Hammond came to visit him in the hospital the last day Paul was there. He brought a *People* magazine and *Sports Illustrated* for Paul to read.

"Thanks so much, Chip." *Not such a bad guy, even if he is a young twerp. Didn't expect any visitors at all.*

After his late-afternoon discharge, Paul still had pain and some swelling in his leg. The doctor gave him strict instructions to take it easy.

Two weeks later, Paul felt better, but the symptoms were still not completely gone. His leg had swelled up again. He was prescribed another antibiotic by the doctor.

Dr. Lanning said, "You will still have residual signs, symptoms, and impairment that could last up to a month. The usual prognosis is eight days of pain, eleven days of extremity edema, and you probably will miss two weeks of work. After that, a full recovery is expected. You probably could resume activities of daily living by the end of October. We will keep in touch. Call my secretary for a follow-up appointment."

Good thing I have COBRA insurance. And I don't have to worry about missing work.

Paul took it easy, resting at his house. He wore an electronic ankle bracelet on his left leg. Chip stopped by occasionally to check in on him. A few times he carried in a sack of groceries under his arm for Paul. Chip informed him that his court case was scheduled in November, probably after Thanksgiving. Paul told Chip how much he appreciated his help while he was recovering.

Carrying a folded *OC Today* newspaper under his arm, Chip popped in to see Paul on November 12. He told Paul the court date was scheduled for the twenty-seventh. Handing Paul the newspaper, Chip said, "Here's something for you to read." His eyes dropped down to Paul's leg. "How are you feeling?"

"Still hurts to walk some. I don't understand it. The swelling goes down, and then it comes back later," said Paul.

"Is the doctor monitoring this?" asked Chip.

"Yes, he said it will take time. I'll be glad when this ankle monitor is removed from my other leg. Anyway, I'm not going to die from this," said Paul.

"Right, of course not. Listen, Paul, I need to know why you didn't show up at our scheduled meeting October first."

"Honestly, I forgot. I was laid off from my job and had to leave my apartment. I was so busy looking for another job and finding another place to live. When I realized I had skipped our meeting by mistake, I panicked and tried to hide from being caught for violating my probation. I guess the judge will throw the book at me now," said Paul.

"I did hear about people at Implant Products being laid off. Do you have a lawyer?" asked Chip.

"Yes, Jim Reynolds. His office is in Ocean Ci—"

"I've heard of him," said Chip.

"Why? Should I be so worried if you want me to hire a lawyer?" asked Paul.

"I think it would be to your benefit to have a lawyer. When we're in court, the state goes first in a violation of probation hearing. I will testify as to what conditions I feel you have violated in your probation agreement. Why did you contact Mrs. Combe and send her that voice mail message? Didn't you realize you weren't allowed to do that as part of your probation agreement?"

"Yes, I did, but I couldn't help it," said Paul. "I thought my first message was a nice one. I was explaining how I truly felt about her, but when she didn't answer the first message, I was livid. I then sent her a voice mail that was not as nice. You know, once we were very much in love. I can't stop thinking about her. I'm still in love with her. I was hoping she would change her mind and wander back to me. Maybe I'm a fool for still loving her. Maybe I'm stupid for still hanging on. I'll never really change how I feel, and I'll never find another girl like her. Ever." Paul lowered his head.

Chip said, "Paul, you have to stop contacting her. She's moved on, and for God's sake, she has a husband now. You have to move on too."

"Well, that's easy for you to say. She's always in my thoughts and in my dreams."

"If you tell this to the judge, he'll probably tell you the same thing I'm telling you."

"Will I have the same judge?"

"Hard to say. If you get Judge Wiseman, I think you'll be lucky. I thought he was pretty fair to you last time," said Chip. "I hope you get him again."

"What happens when someone violated his probation?"

"It all depends," said Chip. "First, the judge has to determine if in fact you really did violate your probation. The consequences usually depend on a variety of factors, such as the seriousness of the violation, whether you've had any prior violations, and whether there are other circumstances that may lessen the severity of the situation."

"What kind of punishment could I get?" asked Paul.

"A probation violation may result in significant penalties, such as heavy fines, extended probation, jail time, or all of the above."

"Oh, that's just great," said Paul. "Maybe he'll sympathize with me because I had a snakebite. I can't wait to talk to Jim Reynolds. He'll help me out on this. I'm sure of it."

<hr />

November 27, at 9:00 a.m., Paul met Chip at the circuit court on West Market Street, Room 104 in Snow Hill, Maryland. The building was constructed in 1742, but since then several additions and renovations, such as a new second-floor courtroom, fireproof vaults, and a new slate roof were added. It was a large red-brick Victorian courthouse and jail. Above and facing the main entrance, a lofty copper cupola stood out noticeably. Paul sat next to Chip waiting for his name to be called.

The judge was not Wiseman. The new judge resembled Clark Kent, with his jet-black hair combed back slick. He brushed a natural curl from his forehead. His blue eyes, square jaw, and bodybuilder physique made him downright handsome, even in his black-framed eyeglasses. He walked into the courtroom looking to be in his forties, about 6' 3," and weighing around two hundred pounds.

Jim Reynolds said to Paul, "You've got a strict judge this time—Judge Fox. I know him well."

Paul shifted in his chair and tapped his foot. He could feel his heart thumping. "How strict?"

"Stricter than the rest. Let's hope for the best," said Reynolds.

Paul stared at the judge. *What's with the curl? All he needs is a red cape.* Paul decided when his turn came to talk, he'd try to tug at the judge's heartstrings.

Judge Fox dealt with two cases before announcing Paul's turn. Finally he announced he was ready for the next case. Chip Hammond stepped forward. "Your Honor, my name is Chip Hammond. I am the probation officer for Paul Simmons. Mr. Simmons was sentenced to one year probation on July 7, and Judge Wiseman ordered him to pay fines, which he has already paid. He has violated his probation by not appearing for his meeting with me on October first and violating two other conditions in his probation agreement."

Judge Fox said, "Not reporting to the probation officer is a substantial violation. I will decide if it is more likely than not that Mr. Simmons committed the violation. Mr. Hammond, would you please tell the court why you feel Mr. Simmons violated his probation?"

Chip Hammond said, "I couldn't say for sure if Mr. Simmons forgot the date of our meeting on October first, but he never called me to explain why he didn't show up. The day before, he said he could make the appointment. I believe Mr. Simmons willfully kept information from me that he was unemployed after August 31 and had vacated his apartment. He lied when I asked him if his address was the same and if he still worked at Implant Products. The conditions in the probation agreement specified that he remain employed. He never told me he was laid off. He never told me his apartment lease was up. He knew I had to know that information each time we met."

Jim Reynolds lowered and shook his head.

"There are police reports of his contacting Mrs. McCombe in many ways. His behavior hasn't changed. Mr. Simmons even admitted to me that he was aware that he was not supposed to contact Mr. or Mrs. McCombe, as ordered by Judge Wiseman at his hearing on July 7. Mr. Simmons was persistent in leaving unwanted texts and a voice mail that was threatening in nature to Mrs. McCombe after his hearing on July 7. He is well aware that Mrs. McCombe is married but still continues to contact her."

"What were these threatening messages?" asked the judge.

Chip read him the last voice mail and asked him to note the last line. "Also, Your Honor, before July 7, the message written in lipstick on the McCombes' mirror when Mr. Simmons broke into their house was threatening. It spoke of revenge. I think it's from a Shakespearean verse. In conclusion, I find it difficult to believe that Mr. Simmons forgot his probation meeting on October 1 because I called him the day before to set up the meeting for the very next day. How could he have forgotten so quickly? I could not get through by phone after he missed his meeting and tried to call him a few days after that without success. His phone did not seem to be working."

The judge said, "I would like to hear Mr. Simmons's version of what happened. Mr. Reynolds, I take it that Mr. Simmons is your client?"

"Your Honor, yes, I am representing Mr. Simmons."

The judge said, "Go ahead, Mr. Reynolds."

"Mr. Simmons was carrying out his sentence as ordered by Judge Wiseman until October 1. From June 9 to September 30, he was honoring his agreement, attending four probation meetings and paying his fines. Mr. Simmons was laid off from his job on August 31 and had to leave his apartment, buy a home, and find employment. He forgot the appointment he made with his probation officer because he was consumed with looking for a job and moving into his new house. He did not willfully skip the meeting with his probation officer. He may have violated the order by leaving a voice mail to Mrs. McCombe; however, I do not feel the probation agreement specifies in detail the *kind* of contact it prohibits. My client would like to speak on his behalf, Your Honor, if you will allow it."

"I will allow it, Mr. Reynolds, but let me address something with you. You've been a lawyer for how many years now? You know very well that no contact with Mr. and Mrs. McCombe means no emails, no voice mails, no visits, no notes, no talking to them, et cetera. Need I say more?"

"No, Your Honor," said Reynolds, bowing his head.

"Now, Mr. Simmons, what do you have to say for yourself?" asked Judge Fox.

"Your Honor, thank you for allowing me to speak. My lawyer is correct about my missing my appointment. He is right about my forgetting the date of my meeting with Mr. Hammond. I was very busy after the settlement on my house, from September 21 to October 1. My mind was so occupied with moving and buying a new car because I had to give up my company car. I also had to purchase furniture for my new house. I didn't think to tell him about my move and job loss because of everything that was going on, but I intended to do so after I got everything settled. I forgot all about my meeting with Chip—I mean Mr. Hammond."

Paul heard something drop on the floor behind him. He turned around and saw Amie and Patrick sitting in the second row. He smiled at Amie and turned around to face the judge.

"Your Honor, I sent the messages to Mrs. McCombe, my former girlfriend, because I wanted to get back together with her. I felt we could still have a chance. We had a wonderful relationship, but she needed more time to think about us getting married."

Amie shook her head.

"Back then, she told me that she needed her space. My focus was on taking care of my mother. I had to take care of her daily because of her having a massive stroke, even though I desired to get back together with Amie McCombe. I care for Mrs. McCombe still. I can't forget her, and I want us to be a couple again. I would never kill her. I wasn't threatening her. I love her so much. I am so sorry I forgot about my meeting and sent messages to Mrs. McCombe. I am so blinded with love for her, I wasn't even thinking about violating my probation agreement."

"May I speak, Your Honor?"

Judge Fox sighed, nodded deliberately, and said, "Yes, Mr. Reynolds."

Mr. Reynolds said, "Thank you, Your Honor. Mr. Simmons didn't mean he was really going to kill Mrs. McCombe in his voice mail message. It was only a figure of speech. For example, saying, 'I'll kill myself if I don't pass that exam' doesn't mean a person would actually kill himself if he failed the exam. It is only an expression that is not to be taken seriously. The other message, about a spanking, is not to be taken literally either. Your Honor, in this particular case, I feel the evidence shows that the violation was not willful in either case. Mr. Simmons acted like a lovesick teenager over this woman, and in his heart and mind, he thought he was doing the right thing."

Judge Fox asked Paul, "Mr. Simmons, is something wrong with your phone? Your probation officer couldn't get hold of you on and after October 1."

Paul said, "Your Honor, my phone wasn't powered around that time. I was so very busy with my new house improvements and chores, that I didn't have time to buy a new charger then."

Judge Fox stared a moment at Paul, shook his head, and then said, "I have to decide if it has been proven that there was a willful violation of probation by the preponderance of the evidence. Mr. Simmons, you were called the day before to attend a probation meeting on October 1, which you said you would attend but forgot. It appears that you have committed an unwanted pursuit of Mrs. McCombe over a period of several months, from what I've heard. And your obsession with contacting Mrs. McCombe didn't stop after you knew it was prohibited in your probation agreement. Your voice mail was threatening in spite of what you said. Stop stalking this woman, Mr. Simmons. You can't have everything you want in life, Mr. Simmons. I'd like to date Katy Perry, but she's taken." Laughter could be heard in the courtroom. "Get over it and move on with your life and end this harassment. I've weighed all the testimony to make my decision. My rationale is, if you haven't done it right the first time, then you won't do it right the second time. I find you guilty, Mr. Simmons, of violating the terms in your probation agreement. I order you to serve sixty days in jail and finish your probation term of one year. I also order you to seek the help of a counselor on a regular basis. Next case."

Chip turned to Paul and said, "I wish you had been honest with me, Paul. You'll have to serve your sixty days first, and I believe that will count toward your probation sentence. You already have served three months of your probation. So if all goes well, your probation period may be over by August 2016."

Paul said, "You really did a good job smearing me, but I guess it's my fault for this mess I'm in. Since I'm not going home, I'll need your help now, Chip. Could you please get my mail for me? I'll need to pay some bills, such as Verizon, and the water and electric bills, while I'm in jail," said Paul. "Here's the key to my PO box. And can you please check on my house from time to time?"

"I'll see what I can do," said Chip. "We can talk about it later."

Paul turned to his lawyer and said, "Can we appeal this?"

Jim Reynolds shook his head. "Mr. Simmons, if you want this to go further, please hire another lawyer."

Amie and Patrick left their seats after Paul was led to a door at the rear of the courtroom. She looked at Patrick. "Well, glad that's over. Thank the Lord. No more laundry list."

Patrick said, "We're going to keep the restraining order active even though he'll be in jail for two months. He'll get out sometime in January. The protective order I filed specifies a stay-away distance of one hundred feet. I hope this teaches him a lesson. He deserves to have—"

Amie's cell phone vibrated in her purse. Her face lit up as she listened and then hung up. "It was Joe. Cici's water broke. She's on her way to the hospital."

Paul had a lot to think about while spending two months in the Berlin Police Jail, a small jail in the historic town of

Berlin, Maryland. Chip brought him his mail every two weeks, though it was only mostly ads. Paul read the junk mail because it filled up his time. He did get a letter from the state that told him that he was ineligible to collect unemployment benefits during the time frame when he was receiving severance payments from his previous job. Paul read that he would be able to collect unemployment benefits when the severance ran out in September 2016 if he still didn't have a job.

Paul decided that he would seek employment when he was released from jail. After thorough consideration, he planned to enroll in the Ed Smith Real Estate School on Sunset Avenue in Ocean City. He would take a real estate practice course, which would qualify and prepare him to take the Maryland Real Estate Salesperson Exam. The tuition and textbook costs were reasonable.

Paul knew about the restraining order the judge had granted the McCombes. The order was in effect for five years. Chip told him that the McCombes could ask the court later to have the order extended to another five years, or permanently if they chose to do so.

If Paul were to enter the real estate business, he knew he'd have to be extra cautious to keep his distance from Amie.

CHAPTER 17

Two Months Later

Amie rocked Lindsay in her arms. "She's so cute, Cici."

"I'm the happiest woman in the world," Cici said. "Joe adores Lindsay. You should see how he interacts with her. And to think he wanted a boy."

"I've seen how he is." Amie smiled. "She'll be her daddy's little girl." Amie kissed Lindsay's forehead. "Look, I rocked her to sleep." Amie looked up at Cici. "So I guess you'll be a stay-home mom now and won't return to work at the shelter for abused women," Amie said.

"Well, not right away," said Cici. "I was emotionally involved in this one case with an abused wife and her children. It reminded me of what I went through with Greg. She had a rocky marriage and was naïve like I was. This woman tried to cope with everything by trying to keep her husband happy and believed for a long time that it was her fault or the children's fault for his violent behavior. He shoved her, kicked her, called her names, and threw things at her. That was just some of it. He isolated her from her friends and blamed her or their children for his outbursts and violent nature. She hid it from the world like I hid my problems with Greg from you. I really wanted to help the poor woman, but in the long run, she had to make the decision by herself to leave him. When she told me that he threatened to burn their house down with her and the children inside, I called Joe for help and contacted the Domestic Violence Center. She finally found the courage to leave him. She thanked all of us for our support. The family court ordered him not to contact the children under any circumstances. I just wonder how she's doing now."

Amie said, "That's a nightmare. She went through hell."

Patrick entered their sunroom. Amie looked at her watch. "Can I hold her?" Patrick asked.

"Not now. I just got her to sleep. You're home early. How was your day?" asked Amie.

"We had a grandmother scam today."

"A grandmother scam?" asked Cici.

"Yeah, a seventy-seven-year-old woman called us today about a phone call she received. She was sort of frantic, and I calmed her down so I could understand what she was saying. Apparently, this guy called her and said that he had kidnapped her granddaughter. He told her he wanted $5,000 and would call her back to tell her where to send the money. He threatened to harm her granddaughter if she called the police or the parents of her granddaughter and said he would return her as soon he had received payment. So I drove over to her house, and I entered through the rear door just in case the scammer could be watching the house. I talked to her a bit more to reassure her that it was probably a scam and that this happens a lot."

"Really? It happens often?" asked Amie.

"Yes, believe it or not. These scammers can sometimes make $10,000 a day. They call senior citizens impersonating a grandchild in distress, begging for cash. Senior citizens are robbed of roughly $3 billion a year in financial scams. A lot of these scams are run outside the US."

"How did he know she had a granddaughter?" asked Cici.

"Con artists usually buy their victim's personal information online, including age and income. People over sixty-five are targeted, mainly because they're more gullible. The elderly are more accessible, and once the con artist gets them emotionally involved, they'll do what the scammer asks."

"So what happened?" asked Amie.

"If he called her back, I wrote down what she was to say to him before she hung up. Anyway, her phone rang about forty-five minutes after I arrived, and the scammer told her to send the $5,000 to a bank account in Virginia. She asked the scammer to please return her grandchild, because she had diabetes. He said he would as soon as she deposits the money into the bank account. He proceeded to give her instructions. I could hear what he said. The elderly woman asked to speak to her granddaughter, and he said that she was in the bathroom. She then asked him if he could tell her the color of her granddaughter's hair. If the scammer really had her teenage granddaughter, he couldn't help but see she had predominantly neon-purple-dyed hair. He didn't answer the question and said to her if she didn't send the money, she'd never see her grandchild again. The elderly woman said she would send it and hung up. She did a great job acting out her role. I contacted the bank in Virginia and gave them the lowdown. Long story short, the Virginia authorities arrested him because the bank agreed to make it look like she had deposited the cash. They nabbed him when he came in to collect the money."

"Oh, the miracles of technology," said Cici.

"Was he from this country?" asked Amie.

"Yes. He's only twenty-eight years old and is now in federal custody awaiting sentencing," said Patrick.

"Wow. Anything else happen today?" asked Amie.

"Not much else except my spying on a cheating wife."

"Cheating keeps your business rolling," said Cici.

"Yeah, it does," Patrick said, scoffing. "I did check with Chip Hammond to see how our friend Paul is doing. Apparently he'll be living in the same little shack, and he'll be looking for a job after he's released from jail. Chip said he was aware of the restraining order's circumstances and said he didn't want to go back to jail ever again. He'll be released at the end of this month."

"I'm glad you're keeping an eye on him," said Amie.

Whimpering could be heard.

"Ooops, Lindsay's awake," said Amie. "Cici, I wanted to tell you earlier, before Patrick came home, that he and I are trying now to have a baby."

"Seriously? That could be so cool. Our kids could be playmates," Cici said.

"I know." Amie grinned. "Cici, was labor really that painful?"

"Yes. For me it was, anyway. I was so glad when my OB/ GYN doctor gave me an epidural. Before that, he told me to stop screaming like a cow. I hate him for saying that. I'm changing doctors. He should have gone through what I experienced. I'd bet that he'd squeal like a pig."

Amie broke out laughing. "Cici, you're too much."

"Well, I have to go home. Hand me my little one," said Cici.

"Not before I hold her a sec," Patrick said.

"OK, just for a minute. It's time for her feeding," said Cici.

⚔

Paul's release from jail on January 27 couldn't have come fast enough. He was given his watch and wallet when he checked out. Chip was waiting for him in his car outside in front of the Berlin Jail. Paul gazed up at the blue sky, put his hands on his hips, deeply inhaled the fresh air, and waved at Chip.

"Thanks for taking me home," he said. "And thanks for everything you've done for me while I was in jail. Getting my mail and checking on the house was a big help. At least my credit record will remain good," said Paul.

"You're welcome. When we get to your house, we can discuss a few things and set up a schedule of our meetings. I brought you a 2016 calendar to record our appointments each month, and I want to talk to you about seeing a counselor."

"OK," said Paul.

"Yeah, and get in touch with me if you can't make your meeting this time," said Chip.

"Absolutely. It won't happen again."

Chip pulled his car around to the front of Paul's house. When they got out, Paul wanted to walk around his house to give it an inspection. "Wait a sec." After going around the back of his house, he then walked around to the front and entered the screened-in porch, where Chip was waiting for him.

"Looks fine so far. Better than jail," said Paul. Both men walked into the living room. "It's nice and warm in here. You must have turned up the heat for me," said Paul.

"Yep. I had it on fifty-five degrees when you were gone and set it yesterday on sixty-eight," said Chip. "There's a few groceries in the fridge."

"Thanks again."

They sat down, Chip in the rattan chair and Paul in the leather club chair. Chip gave Paul the name of the counselor Judge Fox had ordered him to see. Paul glanced at the business card in his hand. "Ruth Collins," he said aloud.

"She's very good," said Chip. "A lot of my clients like her. I set up your first meeting with her next week on February 5. When do you think you'll start looking for work?"

Paul said, "I'll start this week. I want to find something before the end of the summer, because I'll receive no more paychecks after September."

"I'd like to check with you each week to see if you're having any luck finding something," said Chip.

"No problem, but it will take some time, especially when I fill out an employment form disclosing that I broke the law and was in jail."

"That's true, but if I can do anything to help, let me know."

"I'm pretty sure I'll receive good recommendations from my old boss," said Paul. "And from my former coworkers from Implant Products."

"That's the first step," said Chip.

After Chip left, Paul rummaged in the fridge for something to eat. He then sat down in his rattan chair and munched on some Gouda cheese and pondered whether he should walk over to the River Run Golf Course and pick up his Honda or thumb a lift on Racetrack Road to get his car.

Paul's car started up right away. *Good ol' Honda*. He turned left on Route 589 toward Ocean City. He stopped at Walmart and bought a pair of high-cut backpacking boots with excellent ankle support and stiff midsoles. He'd throw out his flimsy old rubber boots. Paul tossed the bag containing his new purchase into the trunk of his car. He'd wear the boots if he hiked in the woods, protecting his legs from prowling snakes.

Paul headed to Sunset Avenue and registered for the spring course to get his real estate license. He knew if he were to become a real estate salesperson, he would be asked to disclose any actions that had been illegal and also disclose the fact that he had a conviction on his record. He would wait until later for that. He wanted to see if he liked the course first. He knew that the state of Maryland would ask for the information to be disclosed on his application to sit for the real estate exam. If they knew he had paid his debt to society and could exhibit honesty, integrity, and trustworthiness, he might be able to get the opportunity to start over with a new career with unlimited income potential.

Paul had given serious thought to future plans after his time was up in jail. He reluctantly decided to sell his house. He was sad about his decision. But staying there with Amie nestled in the woods, away from everyone, was a highly unlikely plan now. Patrick and Chip knew where he lived. He'd have to sell his property and find an apartment or condo to rent again.

He called Coastal Auctioneers and asked them for the contact number of the auctioneer, Walter Crane, who had sold him the house. They gave him his number, and Paul was able to reach him on his cell phone the next day.

"Mr. Crane, this is Paul Simmons. Back in August, you sold me the house on the one-acre lot near Ocean Pines."

"Oh yes, I remember. You beat a couple to the punch at bidding on that house. How can I help you?" Crane asked.

"Well, I was curious to contact them, because they were very interested in the property, and I wanted to see if they would like to purchase it from me. I think their last name was

Dillon. Is it possible you have information on where I could contact them?"

"I can look and see…Not sure, but my secretary may have saved the registration forms. I'll check. Why do you want to sell it?"

"I thought I'd be able to build a bigger house on the lot, but I was laid off from my job, and I'm unable to make such a big investment now."

"Oh, sorry to hear that. Let me see if we have their address. I'll call you back if I find out how you can get in touch with them."

"Thanks," said Paul, and he made sure that Crane had his number.

⚔

Auctioneer Crane called back and gave Paul the Dillons' phone number. He also told Paul that the Dillons lived in Salisbury. Paul thanked them after Crane wished him good luck. Paul immediately dialed their landline number.

Ari Dillon picked up on the first ring.

"Mr. Dillon, this is Paul Simmons. I'm the person who bought the property you and your wife were interested in back on August 7. I've hit on hard times, and I lost my job. I had plans like you and your wife had…to build a larger home on that acre of land, but I'm unable to do that now. I plan to put the house on the market, but I was wondering if you and your wife would still be interested in buying my property at a lower price than what I paid for it. I wanted to let you know before I put it on the market."

"How did you know we wanted to build on that lot?"

"I was standing near you and overheard your conversation with your contractor before the bidding opened."

"Oh. Well, I can't give you an answer now. I have to talk to my wife. You said you'd give us a lower price than what you paid for it? What price were you thinking?"

"Thirty thousand," said Paul. "You know it's worth more."

"Give me your number, and I'll get back to you after I speak to my wife."

"Certainly," said Paul, and after giving Ari his number, he hung up.

A few days went by, and Paul did not think the Dillons were interested in purchasing his property. But to his surprise, they called back and said they would be interested only if they could take another look at the property. They also wanted to bring their contractor with them. If all was sound, he said they would buy it for $25,000 and no more.

Paul agreed to his offer.

After inspecting the property, the Dillons purchased Paul's house. They were thrilled. Settlement was scheduled in one month, on April 3. Paul contacted Jim Reynolds to accompany him when the settlement took place at the title company.

Paul met with Ruth Collins, his counselor. She worked at Delmarva Psychologists in Berlin. Her space was shared with another psychologist. Plenty of sunlight filtered through the blinds in the reception area. After she introduced herself to Paul in the waiting room, she asked him to come into her cozy office and sit down on the small sofa while she took a seat in a wing chair opposite him. Her walls were painted a pale yellow, and she had fresh flowers in a glass vase on her desk. Her brunette hair was pulled back in a clip, and she wore black pants and a green poncho over a white blouse. Paul estimated her age to be in her midthirties. She slid her eyeglasses to the edge of her nose and looked out over them, peering up at Paul.

"Please feel comfortable calling me Ruth. Is it OK if I call you Paul?"

"Of course, please," he said.

"Let's start by you telling me a little about yourself," she said.

Paul told her about his family life growing up in Salisbury, his job layoff, his relationship with Amie, and why he was on probation.

"Do you still want to contact Amie?"

"I know I can't. I'll go back to jail, but I do want to move on with my life. I sold my house and will be looking for an apartment or condo in Ocean City." He then told her about the course he was taking in real estate.

"That will keep you very busy. It's a lot of hard work," she said. "My mother was a realtor, and I know the long hours were difficult for her, but she loved her job."

The hour flew by, and Paul felt at ease talking with her. He was scheduled to meet with her weekly.

⚓

When April rolled around, Paul arranged for Fenwick Marina to haul his boat back to the rickety pier and secure its lines to the pilings. Paul was pleased to see that more planks had been replaced, and it was much safer to walk on the boards. He was looking forward to cruising on the Saint Martin's River again.

On April 3, Paul met Jim Reynolds at the title company in Ocean City with Mr. and Mrs. Dillon. They were wearing smiley faces when they walked into the title company's conference room. Everyone was cordial, and Susan Dillon was especially overjoyed. They also brought a lawyer with them to oversee the financial calculations.

Susan said, "I can't wait to begin our dream of rehabilitating animals and releasing them into the wild. We'll care for those who don't fully recover and keep them for their lifetime. We want to build a large home with a huge front porch and call our place Susan's Rescue Farm."

"What kinds of animals do you plan to care for?" asked Paul.

"Deer, squirrels, bunnies, raccoons, opossums, horses, blue jays, goats, owls…you name it," said Ari, smoothing each side of his mustache with his index finger and thumb.

"We'll need to have our contractor build pens, cages, and, of course, fences for the animals to roam around safely," said Susan.

"You certainly are real animal lovers," said Paul. *But watch out for the copperheads.*

The closing went without difficulty. Jim Reynolds saw to it that the figures on the settlement sheets were correct. Paul thanked Reynolds and paid him for his efforts and time. He shook Ari Dillon's hand before leaving and shoved the certified $25,000 check into his pants pocket.

A week later, Paul looked at a few condominiums in Ocean City and found one unit to rent that he liked. He decided it would be better to rent a unit in a condominium rather than purchase one at this time. The unit was on the third floor in a building on Coastal Highway. Composed of 840 square feet, it was a little bigger than his tiny house. It had central air conditioning and off-street parking. The laundry room was shared, and the building didn't have an elevator. The monthly rent would be worth it to schlep his laundry basket down to the first floor and back up again.

Paul took some of his mother's stored furniture and arranged it in the combined living-dining room area in his condo. He also furnished the bedroom with her king-size bed and bureau. The other bedroom would serve as his office. Life would be good again.

CHAPTER 18

Amie and Patrick docked their pontoon at the side of their long pier. "What a nice day to go out in the boat," Amie said. "I can't believe it's almost May. It'll soon be a whole year since I first encountered Paul."

Patrick said, "It looks like he's taking his probation meetings and the restraining order seriously."

"You said you were going to check on him from time to time," said Amie.

"Yes, and I have, like I said I would," he said, wrapping the line around the piling adjacent to the pier. "I talked to Chip Hammond two days ago. Paul sold his house and lives in Ocean City now, in an apartment or condo. So he's farther away from us since he sold his rattrap of a house."

"Glad to hear it," said Amie. "Thanks for continuing to watch him."

"Don't worry, Amie. I'm on it. I want to protect you more than anything from that lunatic."

"I never noticed his house for sale on the internet," said Amie.

"Chip said it was a quick and private owner's sale. It probably will show up on the internet eventually," said Patrick.

"I'll check. Who bought it?" asked Amie.

"Chip told me that some people bought it who were really into taking care of animals."

"What do you mean?" asked Amie.

"Apparently the people who bought his property are making it into a rescue farm for animals."

"Oh. That's nice. Are the people going to live in that shack of his?"

"I don't know, Amie."

⚔

On Memorial Day, Patrick's office was closed. It was a beautiful sunny day, especially when the temperature reached into the low eighties with no humidity. "It's early. Let's head to the beach," Patrick said. He and Amie packed their towels and beach gear and drove over the Route 90 Bridge to the private Ocean Pines Beach Club. The clubhouse was a three-level cedar shake building containing a snack bar with live entertainment, a pool, volleyball courts, and bathroom facilities. The private facility covered the ocean-side block of land between Forty-Ninth and Fiftieth Streets.

While in the car, Amie glanced over the bridge's guardrail and saw numerous boats cruising in the Assawoman Bay. The sun filtered through the clouds, and the water was clear as crystal. After arriving at the Beach Club, they walked the narrow, sandy path to nab a spot on the beach and unloaded the cooler, towels, and beach chairs. It was crowded, but Patrick finally found a place near the lifeguard's stand and walked back to rent an umbrella while Amie sat waiting for him in her beach chair.

Patrick planted the beach umbrella deep in the sand, and Amie moved her chair under it to get in the shade. They sat together watching the kids playing at the edge of the water.

"I'm getting warm," said Amie. "Let's go in the ocean." At the water's edge, they watched a boat drift by with a sign advertising Dead Freddie's Island Grill.

"I'm going in," Patrick said. He ran and jumped into the water.

Amie remained back, letting the waves at the edge of the shoreline roll over her toes. Patrick waved to her to come in. She shook her head. "I have to get used to it. It feels cold."

The lifeguard blew his whistle. Amie stared at the lifeguard, who was waving everyone to come out of the water. "Patrick, get out of the water!"

The lifeguard had seen a dorsal fin and alerted the beach patrol. Patrick hurried out of the ocean as fast as he could as a wave pounded him on his shoulders. The beach patrol efficiently swept the surf clear of swimmers about two blocks ahead, most of whom didn't need to hear the order of the beach patrol to evacuate.

Dripping wet and a bit out of breath, Patrick pointed. "Look at those teenagers on their boogie boards over there."

The lifeguards raced down to the edge of the water, blowing their whistles, when the shark appeared to be heading toward the boogie-board boys. The guards managed to get the boys to safety as the shark traveled south along the shoreline close to the beach.

After a while in the afternoon, brave vacationers headed back into the water as soon as the lifeguards and beach patrol were certain the shark had moved away from the Ocean Pines Beach Club area. The beach patrol tracked its progress up and down the coast, clearing swimmers from the water as it approached. The shark glided harmlessly along the coastline and was sighted near the long Ocean City pier, and eventually it traveled into the inlet. When the rest of the swimmers in Ocean City heard the news, they flooded back into the surf to resume their normal vacation fun.

Patrick walked over to the lifeguard's stand. "How big do you think he was?" he asked.

"He looked to be about six or seven feet long. I believe it was a hammerhead. The shark may have been hurt. Last week it was tracked to Bethany Beach and didn't really pose a threat. The shark intrigued the beachgoers by gliding only yards off the beach. I think it made multiple attempts to beach itself up there. Strange behavior, swimming up near the surface. Something apparently is wrong with it."

"That's unusual behavior," said Patrick. "I thought that normally hammerheads were not a danger to swimmers."

"Well, you never know," said the handsome, tanned lifeguard. "Don't want to take that chance. It appeared not to be in a hurry to leave. You're right, though. It's fairly abnormal behavior."

Amie walked over to Patrick and said, "Do you want to go back into the water?"

"It's past lunchtime. I'm hungry. I think we've had enough excitement for the day. Let's open the cooler and eat our packed lunches instead," Patrick said.

The sunlit clouds drifted across the blue sky, and Amie and Patrick enjoyed the gentle breeze as they finished their sandwiches.

There was little hope of capturing the ill shark.

When Patrick arrived home four evenings later and walked into his dining room, he saw candles lit and Amie's grandmother's fancy china on the table set for two. Amie was making pot-and-pan noises in the kitchen.

"What's going on, Amie? What's the special occasion? Did I forget an anniversary or birthday?" asked Patrick.

"No. I hope you're hungry. Go wash your hands and get settled. I fixed you your favorite. Pot roast," said Amie.

Patrick did as he was told with a smile on his face. When he came back, Amie had a bowl of Caesar salad and the dish of pot roast resting on the center of the table. "Sit down."

"You're up to something," said Patrick. "What do you want?" He laughed.

Amie's face was radiant. Her smile was captivating. "I'm pregnant."

Patrick rose from his chair and wrapped his arms around her. "That's the best news ever. I'm so happy. What a great surprise." He kissed her, and she beamed.

"Now sit down and eat before I have to warm it up in the microwave," said Amie.

"So that's why I don't see a wine glass for you," said Patrick.

"Oops. I forgot your bottle of shiraz." She retrieved a bottle from the wine cooler and poured him a glass.

"Salud." He clinked her tumbler of raspberry club soda. "You're making me feel like I'm the one having the baby," said Patrick.

"Well, you're the one who gave it to me," she said.

CHAPTER 19

Paul informed Chip that he was enrolled in a real estate course to get his Maryland license at the Ed Smith Real Estate School in Ocean City.

"What are you thinking?" asked Chip. "You know Amie McCombe is a realtor. Are you planning to work at Cathell Realty if you get your license?"

"No, of course not. If I'm accepted, and if I pass the exam, I plan to work for a brokerage firm in Ocean City, not Ocean Pines."

"You still might bump into each other. I don't think it's a good idea," said Chip.

"I will not get anywhere near her if I get this job. Do you realize how many properties are for sale just in Ocean City alone?"

"She could have a client in Ocean City, you know," said Chip.

"I'm not going to worry about that. I will be extra careful and keep away from her."

Chip said, "I'm going to have to tell the McCombes what you're planning to do."

"That's fine. It's even a good idea. I have to find a job, Chip. I'm sure a judge would understand."

"I still don't like the idea," said Chip.

"I may not even get hired because of my background. Incidentally, since you didn't answer my question, there are nine hundred properties for sale in Ocean City right now and 350,000 vacationers on the weekends, creating lots of rentals and condos to buy…too many to count."

"OK Paul, it's your life."

After Chip hung up, Paul left his condo to drive to Salisbury to see Tim.

"Long time, no see, pal," said Tim. Paul and Tim were drinking their beers on the outside deck at the Market Street Inn in Salisbury.

"Glad we could get together. Are you still working at the gym?" asked Paul.

"No. I actually got a real job as a pharmaceutical rep. It's an interesting position, and my experience at Implant Products afforded me a solid background for it. I persuade physicians, this time, to prescribe the company's drugs to their patients. I also educate doctors and other medication-prescribing professionals on new developments in the industry," said Tim. "It took a while to find this job, but it was worth the wait, and I like what I'm doing."

"Congratulations, Tim," said Paul.

"What about you? Did you find a job yet?" asked Tim.

"Sort of. I'm getting my real estate license," said Paul.

"Really? Never would've thought. If you don't mind my asking, how much can you make in that business?"

"Well, I haven't started yet, but to give you an idea…say a house sells for $385,000. The commission at 6 percent on that house would be about $23,000. Top producers can make $100,000 a year."

"Don't you only get a portion of that commission and have expenses to pay as an independent contractor working for a brokerage firm?"

"Oh yeah, and I'll have start-up expenses, like buying my own business cards, for sale signs, advertising expenses, dues, and gas."

"You'll be putting in a lot of odd hours and won't get paid on a regular basis if you have to wait for your commission after the house sells, right?"

"Yeah, but Tim, I'll be getting the money eventually, and I like that it will give me a lot of flexibility. I realize it'll be challenging and a lot of hard work."

"Well, I wish you good luck, Paul. You deserve it," said Tim.

"Did you see Matt's latest email?" asked Paul.

"Yeah, I did. The one where he said he's liking his job, and Sally starts her full-time teaching position in the fall?" asked Tim.

"Yes. Glad to hear things worked out well for them." Paul hesitated to sip his beer. "Are you still dating Kim?"

"No, I'm dating someone else now. It's getting serious," Tim said as he smiled.

"That's great," said Paul. "So you don't mind if I give Kim a call?"

"No, I don't mind at all. Have at it." Tim gave Paul her number.

"Thanks, bud," said Paul.

He called her that evening.

‒

Paul and Kim were making out in the back seat of his Honda Accord. One thing led to another, and they had sex in his car parked in a church lot on Route 589.

"I loved feeling you on top of me," said Kim.

After their lovemaking session, Paul drove to his condo in Ocean City, and he asked Kim if he could take nude photos of her.

"What are you going to do with them?" she asked.

"Keep them for myself," he said. "What else would I do with them?" He scoffed. He poured her a gin and tonic and one for himself.

"I wouldn't want you to be sending them to my new boss or anyone else over at Ortho-Designs," said Kim.

"What do you take me for? Of course not," he said. *What a joke. Almost every good-looking guy at her workplace has probably seen her naked anyway.* "You can trust me, Kim. You have a lovely body, and when I'm not with you, I'll look at your nude pictures. It will turn me on. Come on, undress for me."

She laughed. "OK, since you promised not to show the photos to anyone else."

While Paul sat on the bed, he said, "Start with your blouse." She slowly unbuttoned her blouse. It fell to the floor. Paul got off the bed and nibbled on her bra strap. "You're a goddess," Paul said. She unzipped her skirt, and Paul slid it down her legs. She turned around in her thong, showing off her firm ass. Paul grabbed her hips.

"Don't touch. Just watch," she said. She walked over to the bedroom's doorway and slowly slid her body up and down the doorframe. She moved gradually and steadily. Kim caressed her thighs and licked her lips. She moved her hips from side to side as she bent her knees and straightened up again. She removed her bra and then her thong. She then flipped her hair but remained in her heels. "I'm going to remove your clothes." She gently squeezed his groin.

Paul said, "Let me help you undress me."

He finally gave in and roughly grabbed her. "You driving me insane," Paul said.

After they were done, Paul took about nine nude photos of her and a few selfies of them smiling after they put their clothes back on.

⚐

Paul's next meeting with Chip was a routine one. This time Chip wanted to see his new place, and he met Paul on the steps in front of Paul's condominium building. Chip got a tour of Paul's rented third-floor condo unit. Chip scribbled down Paul's new two-bedroom, two-bath address on Coastal Highway in his notes. He had a few questions for him.

"What is the make of your car?" asked Chip.

Paul told him he was driving a used Honda Accord that he had purchased from his friend, but he needed to get a new registration form and a license plate.

"Anything new in your life? Are you enjoying the real estate course?" asked Chip.

"Yes and yes," said Paul. He showed Chip the selfie he had taken of Kim and himself.

"She's attractive," said Chip. "I'm glad you're dating someone. Where did you meet her?"

"She works at Ortho-Designs. Kim Archer is her name. She was one of the workers not laid off at Implants." *Now Chip will get off my back. He'll think I'm no longer interested in Amie.*

"And to answer your second question, the real estate course is interesting, but a lot is involved. I didn't know that once I pass my exam, I need to take both state and national board exams. Also, there are dues involved, desk fees, technology fees, and insurance. But I could still make money just by selling a decent house once a month. I'm sure I'll sell more than that. There's a lot of knowledge to absorb, but I should be finished by the end of June. I think it's an exciting line of work. I'm spending a lot of time applying myself and hitting the books."

"Glad you find it likable. Are you able to get by for a while until you start your career? You know you have to wait to be paid until settlement on your houses."

"Chip, my finances are fine. The rent is only $600 a month, and I saved most of my severance pay. I'm not worried about my money situation at all." *Jim Reynolds should be finished working on my will, so if anything happens to me, Amie will inherit my money. Maybe I'll leave a portion to Chip. Wouldn't he be surprised.*

"Good to hear you're not worried about money problems, then," said Chip. "You have a nice condo, but the noise in the summer on Coastal Highway will drive you nuts."

"It's better than the shack I had," said Paul.

CHAPTER 20

Amie was bushed after teaching her 4:00 p.m. Zumba class at the community center. She walked over to the parking lot and got into her Mini Cooper. She let out a long breath and turned on her car radio and set it on the Wave. She didn't see Paul parked in his Honda two rows behind her.

When Amie got home, she told Patrick that she was too tired to fix dinner.

"No problem. I'll fix us an omelet. I spoke to Chip today about Paul."

"Oh no," said Amie. "I hope this is good news."

"He told me that Paul signed up for a real estate class in Ocean City."

"What? You're kidding."

"He said that he was against it but really couldn't keep Paul from doing it. He also said he has to pass a background check for acceptance before taking the real estate license exam."

"I can't believe this," Amie said. "He has to be getting his real estate license to get closer to me."

"According to Chip, Paul mentioned again that he would not get anywhere near you. He also told me that he now has a girlfriend," said Patrick.

"I don't believe it," said Amie. "I'm still going to have to watch my back again," she said.

"And I'm still going to keep real close tabs on him," said Patrick.

At work the next morning, Amie sat at her desk, trying hard to engross herself in reviewing the new listings in Ocean Pines. She flinched when a coworker suddenly entered her office and walked in behind her desk.

"Sorry," she said. "I didn't mean to scare you."

"It's OK." Amie updated her on the latest news about Paul and about the restraining order. "Guess I should let everyone know his future plans and where he lives now."

Amie felt she'd have to go back to having someone with her when she showed an open house. *I can't live this way.*

At lunch, Amie met Cici at Taylor's Neighborhood Restaurant near her realtor's office.

"How are you feeling?" asked Cici.

"Good. No morning sickness at all," said Amie.

"I hope it's a girl," said Cici.

"I know. It would be nice for Lindsay to have a playmate, but I don't want to know the sex of my baby. Unlike you, I really want to be surprised," said Amie.

"A Christmas baby," said Cici. "If it's a girl, it could be Holly, Mary, Noel, or Joy. If it's a boy, it could be Christian, or Mark, John, Peter, or Luther."

"Don't make me laugh," Amie said.

"Notice I didn't say Paul," said Cici.

Amie threw her napkin at her.

❧

Patrick and Joe Crabbe took turns following Paul. It was boring work, but at least Paul wasn't driving in or around the Ocean Pines area. He was spending most of his time between Ocean City and Salisbury. Patrick and Joe witnessed him with his new girlfriend several times at Belly Busters and at the Blu Crab restaurants. They also observed that his girlfriend spent the night a few times at Paul's new place, and Paul spent a couple of nights at her condo in Salisbury. They both found out that he regularly attended the real estate school weekly on Coastal Highway. The times he wasn't at school or with Kim, he was at home in his condo. After three and a half weeks of spying on Paul, they felt Amie was safe from him and stopped their surveillance.

⬧

Kim and Paul untangled themselves in bed, and Kim kissed his lips. "I wish you hadn't been laid off. I think that it was a rotten thing that company did to its employees."

"Me too, Kim," said Paul. "But I am enjoying my—what the hell was that noise? Did you hear that? It sounded like someone screaming," said Paul.

"No it didn't. It sounded like a funny kind of laughter," said Kim.

"I know there aren't any dogs on this floor. The condominium association has the standard rule of one cat or one dog of 'gentle disposition,' whatever that means."

"It didn't sound like any dog I know," said Kim.

Paul got out of bed and slipped on his white terry cloth robe.

"I wouldn't worry about it. It's probably nothing." She tapped his pillow. "Get back in bed with me," she said.

Paul kept his robe on, walked into his kitchen, and made himself a Bloody Mary. He walked back into the bedroom with his drink and stayed in bed with Kim.

Later, Paul stopped by the manager's office and spoke to him about the strange sound he had heard. The manager said, "Oh, so you've heard it too. I've received complaints from several people in units on the second and third floors that they've heard unusual noises also."

"What are you going to do about it?" asked Paul.

"Well, I left a message with the resident and inquired if any other owners in the building heard the strange sounds and knew what the cause was. He hasn't called me back, and a few of the members on the condominium board here insist on my finding out what's causing the noises. They are positive it's coming from his unit, at the end of your hall. I'm going to check it out as soon as he comes home from work this evening."

After Paul spoke to the manager, he climbed up the steps to the third floor and put his ear to the resident's door at the end of the hall. He heard nothing and headed back to his condo.

"Did you find out what the noise was?" Kim asked.

"No, but the manager is investigating it."

Kim asked Paul to spend the night at her condo in Salisbury.

Paul said, "I can't, Kim, but I can come over tomorrow night if that's OK. I want to see if I hear any more ruckus on my floor."

Kim slipped on her sweater. "See you tomorrow," she said, and she left for Salisbury.

Paul was awakened at 2:00 a.m. by the screaming noise again. He confronted the manager for the second time the next morning and said, "Let's go upstairs together and knock on the guy's door."

The manager said, "I was just about to head up there. I missed seeing him yesterday. I want to get to the bottom of this before the next board meeting. I checked outside in the parking lot, and his car is still here."

They climbed the stairs and rapped loudly on the resident's door. It was clear when the occupant opened his door that he was not pleased with the intrusion.

"What do you want?" he said. "I have to leave for work right now. This is not a convenient time to come."

But it was too late. Over the resident's shoulder, the manager and Paul caught sight of at least two chimpanzees prancing around the unit. They were attired in diapers and seemed excited at seeing the visitors. It was an awkward moment.

"So those two monkeys are the reasons everyone has been complaining," said the manager.

"They're chimpanzees. I need them here with me. They are vital for my research purposes."

"This isn't going to work out," said the manager.

Paul scoffed. "Do you really think you can keep them quiet?" asked Paul.

"I have to caution you. I will report this immediately to the board," said the manager.

Chimpanzee owner said, "Sorry, I have to leave for work. You can let me know what the board decides, and then we'll see what happens."

The following week, the board ordered the resident to vacate the premises immediately with his chimpanzees or get rid of them.

Things remained quiet on the third floor. Paul didn't hear any more screeching or funny laughter after that.

⚐

Paul and Kim sat at the bar at Galaxy 66 in Ocean City, drinking their cosmos and eating from the small-plate menu after having fun flying around on their go-carts in west Ocean City near the Tanger Outlets. While Kim rambled on, Paul looked right through her and wished he were sitting there with Amie. He had enjoyed watching Amie from a distance the other evening as he slumped down in his driver's seat in the community center's parking lot, concealing himself. He was planning to observe her again undetected sometime soon.

On June 21, Paul completed his real estate course. He had spent many hours of his spare time studying like a madcap and was ready to take the license exam. But before Paul could take his exam, the Maryland Real Estate Commission needed to screen his criminal history, which he had disclosed on his application for a license. Jim Reynolds, Paul's lawyer, recommended he obtain a copy of his official Department of Justice criminal background report. Paul was required to get fingerprinted, even though his prints were already on file. Paul started the process because he knew that a criminal conviction was not an automatic disqualification.

Paul was glad that Jim Reynolds had experience in expunging several convictions for people getting their real estate licenses. He told Paul that a properly done expungement can make the difference between his being granted his real estate license and being denied. "Paul, I'm pretty sure I can get your conviction expunged. Embezzlement, grand theft, extortion, forgery, drug possession, tax evasion, assault, murder, et cetera is not the issue in your case. I've seen a criminal with a serious felony on his record get a certificate of rehabilitation and still get his license. And I've known people with lengthy criminal records still get their licenses."

"I appreciate anything you can do for me. It's worth every cent I'm paying you," said Paul.

Paul's day in court went well. Jim Reynolds did an excellent job representing Paul. He had a custom plan devised for Paul. Paul's real estate instructor's comments and recommendations helped his case. Ruth Collins, Paul's psychologist, convinced the judge that Paul was on his way to being sufficiently rehabilitated after nineteen weeks of counseling. And of course, Chip Hammond praised Paul for moving on with his life, explained the changes he was making, and verified how conscientiously he worked on his course studies.

Paul's lawyer was able to expunge Paul's misdemeanor conviction, but Paul still had to keep the conviction on his application for a license and attach a copy of the judge's expungement order to it. Paul and Jim Reynolds were glad they had Judge Wiseman, who had reviewed Paul's case in court and had issued the court order granting it. And the Maryland Real Estate Commission did not deny him his license based on his conviction.

Paul was offered a position at Shark Realty, a small brokerage firm. One week later, he picked up the phone in his brokerage firm's office. On the other end was a client looking for a home on the bay side of Ocean City. Paul was excited—he had his first client just by answering the phone. The house Paul wanted to show the middle-aged couple was in the popular community of Montego Bay, Ocean City, and had a view of Assawoman Bay. It was in move-in condition, had never been a rental, and was close to a canal-front fishing and crabbing area. The community boasted a lot of amenities. The listing price was $260,000. It was a start, and Paul looked forward to showing them the house.

That same day, Tim surprised Paul and asked him if he would show him some condos in Ocean City with a view of the ocean that didn't exceed $300,000. "My girlfriend and I are going to split the cost of a beach house. Can you show us a few, Agent Simmons? We don't want any that are in need of a lot of updating."

Paul laughed. "Absolutely. You guys really must be serious."

Tim chuckled. "Can you give us a discount on the commission?"

"Of course," said Paul.

So many two-bedroom condos with a view of the ocean were on the market. Tim and Jennifer had a lot to choose from among the many units Paul showed them.

⚏

Kim and Paul were relaxing in their Adirondack chairs outside on Paul's balcony. The traffic noise on Coastal Highway didn't bother them. The balcony offered shade, and the weather that evening was quite pleasant. Sipping their dirty martinis, they listened to the cackling as Kim pointed to the V-shaped formation of geese flying by. Paul's cell phone buzzed and rattled on the small glass-top patio table.

"Hey Tim, what's up?" asked Paul. Pause. "Really? That's great. Glad you liked it." Pause. "OK, I'll meet you at my office tonight. What time?" Pause. "Will Jennifer be there? Good. I enjoyed meeting her the other day. She's a beautiful girl." Kim shot Paul a look. "All right. See you at the real estate office at 7:00 p.m."

"That was Tim?" asked Kim.

"Yes."

"What was that about, and who is Jennifer?" asked Kim.

"Tim and his girlfriend are buying a two-bedroom condo they like that I showed them in the Pyramid."

"His girlfriend? He's buying a condo with this girl Jennifer? Why didn't you tell me he had a girlfriend?"

"Why do you care?" asked Paul.

"You could have told me. Tim and I were a couple, remember?"

"I didn't think you'd be interested. Your relationship with him is over," said Paul.

"If we are going to be together, and he's your friend, I don't like you keeping things like that from me. What does she look like? You said she was beautiful."

"She is. She's absolutely gorgeous."

"What? Prettier than me?" asked Kim.

"Kim, knock it off."

"You like her, don't you? I bet you were flirting with her. No wonder they bought the condo. She probably fell under your spell."

The argument got heated. "Tim asked me to show him some properties. Stop being so damn jealous."

"I'm not jealous. I guess you're leaving me to have them sign a contract tonight. Right?" asked Kim.

"It's my job."

Kim raised her voice. "Some job. You're going to be leaving me all the time with your new job. Why couldn't you get a job like you had before? One like Tim has."

Paul felt the anger rise in his chest. He yelled back, "Damn it, if you don't like it, get yourself another guy," said Paul, and he stomped out the front door of his unit, leaving her sitting there with her mouth agape.

Signing papers at the real estate firm where Paul worked took an hour and a half. Paul's rapid-fire barrage of countless papers overwhelmed Tim and Jennifer. Paul helped them by clarifying the terms and conditions in their contract. When the final page was signed, Tim said, "Wow, I didn't realize signing a contract would be so detailed and take this long."

Jennifer asked, "Paul, can you point me to the restroom?"

Tim watched as she disappeared around the corner.

"How's it going with Kim?" Tim asked.

"We had our first fight," said Paul.

"Did you make up?"

"Not yet. She doesn't seem to like the idea that I'm working odd hours now. She was mad that I had to leave and come here," said Paul.

"She was a bit clingy with me," said Tim. "Hope you guys can work things out."

"I'm not upset about it. She's just a date. I'm not making any commitments right now with anyone, especially her," said Paul.

Jennifer walked back into the conference room. While handing Tim their packet of copied pages of the contract, Paul said, "I have a good feeling they'll accept your offer." They all shook hands and left. Paul didn't have to close up the office, because two other realtors were still working down the hall. He let them know he was leaving.

Opening the door to his unit and looking inside, he felt an emptiness fill the room. Kim had gone. When Paul turned his head to the right, he saw a note on the dining room table. It was in Kim's handwriting.

Paul, I'm so sorry for the way I acted.

I am so proud of you for getting your

license. I know how hard you studied and worked to achieve your goal and pass the exam. I care about you more than you know and hope you can forgive me. I love every minute that we are together. Please forgive me.

Paul crumpled up the note and threw it in the wastebasket in his kitchen.

The next morning, Paul headed to his office, which was only five minutes from his condo. He looked at the new listings on the market in Ocean City, Fenwick Island, Bethany Beach, Ocean Pines, and Rehoboth Beach. He familiarized himself with the details of all properties in Ocean City first. Three other realtors were in the office, on their phones with clients. Outside his office, Paul heard the receptionist's phone ring several times. One of the calls she sent back to Paul's office phone.

Paul answered after the second ring. "Hi, Mr. Simmons?" the female voice said.

"Yes, this is Paul Simmons. How can I help you?"

"This is Susan Dillon. I wanted to thank you again for letting us know in advance that you were selling your property. We are making plans for building our house and widening the area by eliminating a lot of the shrubs and trees. It's a real work in progress. The reason I called you is because we have a friend who is interested in buying a home in Ocean Pines on the water. I remembered you were getting your real estate license, and I saw your name listed as an agent for a house for sale in an *O C Today* newspaper recently. Since you were so nice to let us buy your house at a big discount, I gave her your name. She may be calling you."

"That's very kind of you, Mrs. Dillon. Thank you so much," said Paul.

Susan gave Paul her friend's name.

Paul then reviewed information about the new and old listings in Ocean Pines.

⚜

Three days later, Kim waited outside Paul's apartment door, glancing at her Fitbit watch and tapping her foot. It was 8:14 p.m., and she hoped he would arrive home soon. She got her wish, and Paul came out of the stairwell five minutes later and headed to his unit. He saw Kim standing outside his door.

"Hi," she said. "I hope you don't mind my stopping by. May I come in?"

"Of course," said Paul. "I'm in for the night. Let's sit in the living room."

"Your hair's all wet. Is it raining outside?" she asked as she walked toward the sofa.

"No, I just came back from Gold's Gym swimming a few laps," he said.

Kim sat on the sofa opposite Paul.

"Do you want a drink?" he asked.

"No, thank you; not now. We need to talk. I know you got my note of apology. I haven't heard from you since I wrote it, and I just wanted to know how things stand between us. I thought we had a good relationship," she said.

"I agree, we did. I've been busy, but I should have called. I'm sorry."

"Do you want to continue seeing each other?"

"I'd like to take it slow, Kim. I'll be working odd hours, and that includes the weekends. It's the middle of summer, and I know you realize that's our busiest season. Business has picked up and has been good for me, given that I'm new at this."

"I understand. We can work around your schedule, if you like."

"That's fine with me," said Paul.

"Do you want me to stay?" asked Kim.

"Tonight I have a few more work-related issues I have to work on, and I'd rather see you another night." *Not in the mood.*

"OK, I understand," she said. "I dropped in on you un-expectedly and wasn't really anticipating getting together to-night—although it would have been nice." She gave him one of her seductive smiles.

"You're right, but I'll call you, and we'll hook up. Maybe have dinner," said Paul.

"Sounds good." She grabbed her purse and walked out the door after kissing him on the cheek.

CHAPTER 21

Early in the morning, in the kitchen, Patrick heard his cell phone chime and rushed to find it. He discovered his phone in the sunroom between the cushions of the sofa and quickly answered. "Hello?"

"Hey Patrick. It's Hulk. You're gonna like this," he said.

"What's going on?" Patrick asked.

"They arrested a twenty-four-year-old guy for breaking into a house in Paul's old neighborhood in Salisbury. He had tied up the woman in her home while robbing her of jewelry, money, and silver. Thanks to Neighborhood Watch, her neighbor next door saw the guy breaking in through her back entrance, and he dialed 911. I'll cut to the chase…his DNA had matched the DNA taken from the beer can at Mrs. Simmons's house when she was robbed six years ago. Same MO. He was just a kid back then. Get this: he was one of her twelfth-grade math students back when she taught at Wicomico High School."

"Humph. I'll be damned. That's great," said Patrick. "Are you going to tell Paul Simmons?"

"I plan on it," said Hulk, and he disconnected before Patrick could thank him.

Patrick called Amie, who was already at her office, and told her the news. "The first DNA sample on the beer bottle came up empty. No wonder there was no match. The kid had no juvenile or adult record, so he wasn't in any DNA database."

"Well, Patrick, I guess you don't have to be so hard on yourself anymore for not solving who robbed Paul's mother," said Amie.

⚜

Reluctantly, Paul pulled his Honda Accord into the parking lot of the parole and probation office in Salisbury. He climbed up the steps to the second floor and sighed when he reached the door to Chip's office.

"Good morning," said Chip, and he shook Paul's hand with too firm a grip. "Well, it's almost noon, but good morning anyway. I'm anxious to hear all about how the real estate job is going. Sit down."

"It's going very well, thanks." Paul told him about his current listings and sales. "A friend of Mrs. Dillon called me. Remember, she's the lady who bought my one-acre lot?"

Chip remained silent.

"Well, her friend wants a house on the water in Ocean Pines, and Mrs. Dillon referred her to me. So I'm going to show her friend a beautiful waterfront home in the community of Tern's Landing. It's priced in the mid $700,000s, right in her price range."

"Good for you, Paul. Sounds like the real estate business is going well for you. Are you still seeing Kim Archer?" asked Chip.

"Yes, but I'm not ready to make a commitment just yet," said Paul.

"Well, I'm glad you've put Amie McCombe out of your mind," Chip said.

That'll never happen. "Kim and I are going to spend the weekend in Cape May," said Paul. *A little white lie doesn't hurt.*

"Does she understand you don't want to make a commitment right now?"

"Yes, and she doesn't want to rush into anything right now either," said Paul.

After he checked that Paul was still at his same address, he said, "I have some news about your mother's burglar."

"What?" asked Paul, bending his head back and wrinkling his broad forehead.

"Yep, the police nabbed him while he was robbing a home in your mother's former neighborhood. Turns out he was a student in your mother's high school class. He admitted to the detectives that he—I'll quote him—'hated that bitch of a teacher most of all.' Apparently it seemed he was angry she had given him an F in geometry, and it ruined his grade point average. His DNA matched a sample saved from the time back when he burglarized her house. There have been four other robberies in that neighborhood in the last six years, and the police think they can prove he was the one committing all of them."

"Why didn't Patrick McCombe interrogate her students?" Paul asked. "What's his name? When's the trial?"

"Maybe he did investigate them. I don't know the answers to all your questions. I just don't have all that information," said Chip. "Chief Phillips is supposed to be calling you, and maybe he can give you more details."

"My mother would be horrorstruck if she were alive. I'm glad they caught the thug," said Paul. "And I hope they put him in jail for a long time. Patrick McCombe should have been more thorough. The guy was right under his nose."

"I'm positive they'll send him away for a long time," said Chip. "Do you have any other questions?"

"Yeah, as a matter of fact I do, concerning something else. If this new client of mine likes this new home in Ocean Pines, and Amie McCombe happens to show it to one of her clients while I'm there, is that a violation of the restraining order?"

"Good question. For example, if you wound up at the same open house, you would have to leave the premises. You have to be compliant with the order. However, if you and she wound up in the same large restaurant, you could both still eat there, as long as the restaurant was big enough that at least one hundred feet is between you and her. You could even be within visual of each other, but any sort of hollering, eye contact, body language, or any other effort to communicate with her would put you in violation of the order. But it would be your burden to establish that it was truly accidental if Mrs. McCombe complained about your conduct. That's why I was apprehensive about you becoming a realtor in the same zip code as hers. Then again, if this were to happen, she could determine that it's not worth fighting about."

Their meeting ended thirty minutes earlier than usual because Paul asked Chip if he could meet his friend Tim, his former coworker, for lunch.

Smiling warmly, Tim greeted Paul at Burger King in Salisbury. They sat down in a booth that was by a window after carrying their lunches on their trays.

Chomping on his veggie burger with his mouth full, Tim asked Paul if he had made up with Kim.

"We're back together. I don't see her as much because my job keeps me busy, but she's putting up with my odd hours."

"Jennifer and I are looking forward to our settlement. Since we're living together at my condo now, she's splitting the rent with me, and she's going to furnish the beach condo with some of her own furniture, which is really nice. Most of it's from Pier One."

"August is right around the corner, and soon you'll be moving in," said Paul.

"Yeah. We're glad the previous owners wanted to settle quickly, because Jen and I are looking forward to enjoying the beach there before the summer ends."

"I thought you owned your Salisbury condo," said Paul.

"No, I don't own it. I'm renting it," said Tim. "But that severance money went toward chipping in to buy the Ocean City condo with Jennifer."

"Oh. How's the job going?"

"It's great, except I miss the times I had with you and Matt. I'm pretty much on my own and don't have a chance to mingle much with the other reps."

"Maybe in time you'll get to meet more people in your company. Give it a chance. You haven't been there that long," said Paul. He gulped down the last of his diet soda.

"Yeah, I know I will. Tell me how you're doing," said Tim.

In the time remaining before Tim's next appointment, at Peninsula General Hospital, they talked some more about Paul's listings and the standings of the Delmarva Shorebirds. They both slid out of the booth and said their goodbyes. After leaving Burger King, Paul started the engine of his Honda and drove toward Green Acres Memorial Park in Salisbury. He followed a winding road lined with tall cypress trees around to a gravesite.

Sitting on the bench under a sycamore tree overlooking his mother's grave, he began talking to her.

"Mom, I miss you so much. I tried so hard to win Amie back, but she ignores me and doesn't want me to get close to her. I can't understand why she won't give me the time of day. I can't wait much longer. I still love her, even though she resents me. I let you down, Mom. I know you wanted us to get married. I'm sorry. But I'm not giving up…Never. I watch her. She still is as beautiful as the day I met her. I'm dating this other woman to get my probation officer off my back. She can't compare to Amie. No woman can."

He sat quietly a little longer, head lowered, gazing at the ground. Rising from the bench, he told his mom he loved her and left the cemetery grounds, but not before he laid a bouquet of daisies on top of her grave and told her that they had caught her burglar.

Adjusting his tie and combing back his hair after returning from Salisbury, Paul was dressed in his tapered black pants and Ralph Lauren button-down shirt for the Tern Landing's house showing. He parked his Honda on the long brick driveway in front of the incredible five-bedroom waterfront home. As Paul retrieved the listing from his zippered case, his client pulled up in her Mercedes beside his car. Paul got out of his Honda and waited for her to climb out of hers.

Paul put out his hand for her to shake.

"I'm Mrs. Fletcher. Pleased to meet you."

"Likewise," said Paul. He handed her the listing sheet. Her chocolate-brown, deep-set eyes complemented her honey-colored skin. She tucked the left side of her shoulder-length, sable-colored hair over her ear, revealing a sparkly diamond stud. The simple blue denim sheath dress she wore seemed an odd choice for such a classy-looking woman. Paul couldn't guess her age. Maybe late forties or early fifties. *A little too skinny and sophisticated for my taste.*

"The street is really lovely, but the home is gorgeous." She walked around the side of the house to take a peek at the backyard and the water view. "Wow, that's a great view of the Ocean City skyline. Let's go inside."

After opening the lockbox near the front entrance, Paul and Mrs. Fletcher entered the house. She was immediately drawn to the floor-to-ceiling stone fireplace and wet bar in the living room. Paul showed her the waterfront sunroom and large loft area.

"This is really nice. It's all updated too." She ran her hand over the granite countertops in the kitchen and opened the door to a huge pantry.

Paul said, "Did you see the menu-planning desk and the breakfast bar?"

"Yes. This is a great place to entertain."

They went upstairs and saw the private balconies off two of the bedrooms. She walked onto one of the balconies and looked down at the water. Pointing in the direction of the owner's yacht, she said, "My husband will like the private boat dock and lift. I have to bring him here to see this. I can't believe the first house I see, I love."

Paul said, "This one will go fast, so if you want to look at more, you may lose this one. In my opinion, this is the best one in Tern's Landing right now, and the price is reasonable."

"Can we come back later this evening?"

"Of course," said Paul.

"Before dinner and before the sun sets?" She laughed.

Paul smiled and nodded.

Later, after Mrs. Fletcher left, Paul selected a date for an open house of the five-bedroom home with the intention of inviting the realtors in the region to explore the massive house. Even though he was positive he could quickly close the deal on the home with the Fletchers that same evening, Paul needed to have the open house because he was proud of the listing he represented, and he was hoping to see Amie.

⚜

The waterfront home was crowded with realtors on the open-house day. Paul served them lemonade, cupcakes, and smoked salmon dip on crackers, which he spread out on the granite countertop. Many were conversing and looking at the layout of the home and beholding the view of the skyline in the distance from the large deck. Paul introduced himself to several realtors and enjoyed talking to many of them. He kept glancing from time to time toward the front door in the foyer. Then he saw her.

There she is.

Paul saw Amie stroll up the walkway with some guy. He watched as she approached the front entrance, and Paul swiftly headed out the back slider onto the deck. He walked around the side of the house and proceeded toward his car, which was parked on the street. He waited in his car, watching for Amie to exit the front door. Twenty minutes went by, then a half an hour. Amie finally came outside, and Paul immediately started his engine and drove to the end of the cul-de-sac. He observed Amie drive away in her Mini Cooper, and then he returned to his listed house.

Wasn't even missed.

A trickle of realtors surrounded the breakfast bar, munching on the dip and crackers. Others left, thanking Paul. Many were aware that Paul already had a contract on the house, but there was always the possibility that the contract might not go through.

⚰

Amie drove off with Bill Morgan, her friend and a savvy realtor, sitting beside her in the Mini Cooper. "Well, didn't see him," she said. "And thanks for coming with me," she said to Bill.

"Glad to do it," he said. "I didn't see him either." Bill coughed and cleared his throat. "It was a grand house," he said, waving the brochure.

"Yeah, and I wonder how he was able to land that listing. He's fairly new at this."

"Guess he was at the right place at the right time," said Bill.

Amie dropped Bill off at Cathell Realty and drove away to meet with a new client in Bethany Beach. She shook her head. *It didn't work. Really wanted to have him violate his restraining order so he'd be thrown back in jail.*

While waiting on the sofa for Amie to return home from work, Patrick channel surfed until he could settle on something entertaining. At 6:15 p.m., Amie entered the living room as Patrick was changing the channel once more with the remote. Putting the remote down and looking up at her, he said, "Hey, babe, how did it go?"

Amie knew he was referring to the open house and said with a frown, "He wasn't there. My plan to try to have him come closer than one hundred feet was a bust."

"I can't believe I allowed you to talk me into letting you go there, but I felt you'd be OK with Bill by your side," said Patrick.

"I'm glad you did. A lot of people attended, so I wasn't afraid. Too bad my plan didn't work." *What a waste of time that was.*

⚔

The hostess at the Market Street Inn in Salisbury led the two attractive couples to a table in a cozy, romantic, dimly lit corner. Kim had introduced her girlfriend, Diana, and her fiancé, Vince, to Paul after they met in the vestibule of the restaurant. They chatted and drank a couple of cocktails before ordering off the menu.

Paul learned that Vince owned an accounting firm in Salisbury. "How long have you been the owner?" asked Paul.

"Going on eight years…following in my dad's footsteps," said Vince.

Paul nodded.

"Have you decided on a wedding date yet, Diana?" asked Kim.

Paul was immersed in the menu. Kim kicked his foot.

"We want a spring wedding. Maybe April or May," Diana said. "How about you two? How long have you been dating?"

Kim put her arm around Paul and smooched him on the cheek. "Several weeks," she said, and she cuddled closer to Paul.

Paul quickly changed the subject and said, "The Oyster Imperial sounds good. Oysters topped with lump—"

"Oh, I've had that," said Vince. "It was OK. I'm getting the seared Ahi Tuna. Always a winner here."

Kim inched closer to Paul and caressed him. "Aw, don't listen to him, sweetie. Get what you want."

Under their table, Paul felt Kim's hand move up his thigh. He pulled his leg away and gave her a look that made her drop her hand immediately.

The heavyset waitress sauntered over to their table and asked, "Does anyone want another cocktail?"

"Sure," said Kim.

"Drinks all around," said Vince.

They all ordered and then talked more about themselves. Paul yawned and looked at his watch.

Kim asked Paul, "Want to spend the night again at my place?"

Vince couldn't help overhearing and laughed. "I'm sure Paul would love to, Kim."

"You two sound serious," said Diana.

Kim sat there grinning at Paul.

After they finished their meals, Vince patted his belly and exhaled loudly. "I'm too full. No dessert for me."

Kim looked at Paul and said, "I'll be your dessert, honey."

Diana laughed, wiping her mouth with a napkin.

Paul sensed a knot growing in his stomach and felt an urge to smack Kim. He did his best to swallow his discomfort in front of the two strangers.

After splitting the check, they all rose from the table, and Kim and Paul said goodbye to her friends in the rear parking lot.

"Have a good night, you two," Vince said as he cracked up making his way toward his car.

"We sure will," said Kim, giggling and feeling a buzz from her gin and tonics. She rested her head back on the car seat.

The ride home was quiet. Paul stopped the Honda in front of Kim's condo. "Come on up," she said, flickering her eyelashes.

"I don't think so. It's over."

"What?" she said.

"Kim, I want to break up. I'm just not ready for a commitment with you right now. I'm sorry."

"Why? What did I do?" she asked.

"Nothing. I'm just not ready to commit to a relationship. That's all."

Without another word, Kim opened the car door and slammed it shut.

Paul watched her make haste toward her condo, moving in short, quick strides in her spiked heels. *Couldn't stand her clinging to me all night. Don't need or want her anymore.*

CHAPTER 22

Summer was swiftly coming to an end. When Paul opened his mailbox on the first floor of his building, he fixed his gaze on an envelope with Russell and Joan Fletcher's address label attached to its left corner. Paul ripped the envelope open and saw that it was an invitation to a housewarming party in Tern's Landing. He checked his calendar and wrote down the date.

Three weeks later, Paul stood before his full-length mirror admiring how he looked in his outfit. He wanted to look good but not go over the top. Simple and sharp—that was what he wanted. Nothing flashy.

Paul especially wanted to make a good impression on Joan Fletcher's friends. He wore a medium-starched white collared shirt under his black jacket with a clean, dark-blue slim-fit pair of jeans. He was sure people would notice his black leather Gianni Lace Up Cap Toe shoes. He added a leather bracelet, and that was it. *Handsome. Mother would like this combination.* He turned around, checking his hair in the mirror. *Perfect.*

At the front door, Joan Fletcher flashed a big smile as Paul presented her with a bottle of expensive Riesling.

"Oh, how sweet," she said. "Go get yourself a drink at the bar. You look nice."

On his way over to their hired bartender, Paul snatched a cheesy hors d'oeuvre from a tray carried by a cute girl in a mini-skirt. He ordered a Bloody Mary with Old Bay on the rim and took a long sip. Carrying his drink with him, he thought he'd circulate. Lots of people. He blended in with a small crowd outside on the deck looking up at the sky. They were watching a B-25 Mitchell Panchito World War II bomber fly over the house. Someone said, "That must be from the air show at the Ocean City Airport today."

Several people piped in and talked about the different planes they'd seen in past Ocean City air shows. Joan Fletcher walked over with her husband, Russell, while Paul was talking.

"Oh, we see you've met a few of our friends. Everyone, if you haven't met Paul Simmons already, he is the realtor who sold us this wonderful home," she said.

Paul smiled and said, "If anyone is planning on moving, give me a call."

Later, before the party was over, a familiar-looking man ambled over to Paul and said, "Paul, may I have your business card, please? I'm going to give you a call."

Paul remembered him from the plane crowd. "Certainly, Ken. Are you planning to sell or buy?" asked Paul.

"Both," he said.

It was a great party. Treated in luxury.

─⊨─

The second social event for Paul was the Realtors Annual Conference and Expo, held Thursday at the Civic Center in

Ocean City. He didn't want to miss this event. He knew Amie would attend. He was anxious to see her.

The Shark realtors were assembled in a group at the convention. They all agreed to participate in a couple of workshops. One of the workshops would help them keep abreast of the latest and most pressing legal issues facing the real estate sector. They were eager to listen to how to improve their real estate marketing and sales practices. So many brokers, lenders, agents, and techies filled the vast room.

Paul was surprised when he spotted Amie across the way, more than a hundred feet away, at an exhibit stand. She looked so hot. He moved closer. She was conversing with a number of her colleagues, including Bill. *Have to avoid eye contact. Wonder what workshop she'll attend.*

Paul continued to watch her. "Hey, Paul, over here."

He snapped out of his gawking and walked over to one of his coworkers.

"Refreshments," he said. "Come on, let's eat something. Our workshop starts in about twenty minutes."

Paul agreed to indulge. After eating a few tasty snacks, Paul looked back to where he had seen Amie. She had disappeared.

After taking copious notes at an interesting workshop session, Paul thanked the speaker and stayed with his group to attend the next workshop. His mind meandered during the lecture. He had to see Amie. After the workshop, Paul excused himself from the group and searched for her. After an hour, as he headed to the men's room, he found her coming out of the women's restroom. He turned his back to her. *Be careful; I'm too close. This is ridiculous. I can't worry about staying away from her like this for the next five years. According to Chip, I'm supposed to wait until five years is over to be near her, but what if she extends the time another five years? The hell with that.*

Paul walked out of the convention center, hopped in his Honda, and headed to the Bonfire's bar. When he got there, he tried to drown his pain with a few stiff martinis.

At 5:00 p.m., Paul parked his car in the community center's parking lot. He slid down in the driver's seat of his Honda and peered out the windshield, watching Amie come closer to her car after teaching her Zumba class. A row of parked cars stretched in front of his Honda. That and an aisle separated Amie's car from Paul's. Using his binoculars, he had a decent view of her getting into her Mini Cooper, which was nestled between two other cars. It looked as if she was holding something in her left hand.

With her remote in her right hand, she unlocked her car door. She looked over her right shoulder and then to the left. Paul ducked quickly to hide himself further. He counted to ten slowly. He gradually inched back up in his seat and watched her back out of her parking spot and drive off. A woman dressed in sweatpants and a T-shirt walked over to her Jeep, two cars down from Paul's.

I can't keep doing this. I look suspicious. I could get caught. It's time. Time to have a serious talk with Amie. Next week. Time for us to be together.

CHAPTER 23

Early Monday morning, Amie popped into the community center. In the lobby, the receptionist happily greeted her. "Good morning," said Amie. "Is the director here?"

The receptionist said, "Yes, she's in her office. I'll let her know you're here."

Amie smiled at Mrs. Hill, the director of community activities, as she warmly welcomed Amie.

"How are you feeling? How many months left before the baby comes?" she asked Amie.

"I'm doing well, thanks. The baby is due around the end of December."

"You look great, Amie. I thought you'd stop teaching class well before this. Are you planning to leave soon?"

"That's why I'm here," said Amie. "I plan to stop teaching the class after this week."

"I certainly understand. Connie can cover your classes. But we would like you to come back after the baby is born."

"I know. I will. Connie's a natural for it, though," said Amie. "I was lucky I caught you this morning." Amie glanced at her watch. "See you Thursday night," she said.

Amie had to answer Cici's text as she walked to her car.

Call me ASAP.

"Cici, what's wrong?" Amie asked. "Cici?" Amie heard Cici blowing her nose on the other end.

"It's Old Bay. We had to put him down. He couldn't get up to walk."

"I'm so sorry, Cici. He was in so much pain from his arthritis."

"We knew that it was just a matter of time, but Joe is so upset."

"Of course he is. He was such a friendly dog. I know you'll really miss him."

Cici blew her nose again. "We had him cremated. I don't think we'll get another dog. It was so hard to lose him like that. When I go, I'm going to be cremated like Old Bay."

"Believe it or not, I know a friend of a friend who told me her deceased sister-in-law wanted to be buried next to her dog."

"I'm not going to do *that*," said Cici.

"You've lost a member of your family. I can't imagine losing someone so close and special. I haven't experienced losing a dog, but it's got to be so difficult. When Patrick's dad passed away, he didn't want to be cremated, but he wanted a closed casket. He didn't want anyone staring at him when he was lying there in his coffin."

"Not Joe's mom," said Cici. "Joe told me she wanted an open casket and told Joe to make sure he plucked the hairs growing out of her chin so no one would see them before people came to the viewing."

Amie started laughing. "Oh, Cici, you're a piece of work."

Lying in bed in her master bedroom four days later, Amie suddenly placed her fingers in her ears. "Turn that down."

"So sorry. Didn't mean to startle you," Patrick said, turning down the TV's remote volume button. "Didn't realize the volume would be that loud when I turned it on."

"I was already awake, but you woke up our baby," she joked.

They started to watch the Delmarva news on the flat-screen TV before getting out of bed. "Patrick, after I come home from teaching my class, let's go out to dinner."

"Sure. Feel like Italian? We could go to DeNova's."

"Spaghetti sounds good. It'll be my last night teaching Zumba class for a while, so I'll come home and shower, and then we can go out," she said. Amie needed a break from teaching, but she would continue to work at Cathell Realty.

They continued watching the news and turned it off after listening to the cloudy weather forecast. "I hate to get out of bed and go to work. I want to just stay in bed all day."

"I'll get in the shower first," said Patrick. "I'll let you stay in bed for ten more minutes." When Patrick finished showering, Amie rolled out of bed, yawned, and selected her outfit to wear for the day from her walk-in closet.

Leaving work a little earlier than usual, Amie took her time and headed to the community center. When her Zumba class ended that evening, she slipped on her lightweight utility jacket. She grabbed her bright-red Under Armor duffel bag after saying her goodbyes to her students and walked out the front door. Connie followed, and they chatted a minute about Connie covering for Amie while she was on her maternity leave. Amie then waved goodbye and walked to her car.

Amie scanned the parking lot. "Now, where did I park?" She clutched her lipstick spray and put it into her jacket pocket. She headed over to her car, key in hand.

She didn't see him coming as she began to open her car door. "Amie, get into the car."

Amie gasped when she saw Paul pointing his gun at her. "What are you doing?" she asked.

"Get behind the wheel. Open the other side door. I'm getting in the car with you. Remember, my gun is pointing at you.

Amie did as she was told. Her legs were shaky. "Where are we going?" she asked.

"Just drive out of here," he said.

Amie pulled out of the parking lot.

"Keep driving straight. Then when you get to the light, turn left. And at the next light, turn right onto Racetrack Road."

Amie's heart was beating rapidly. *I bet he's going to take me to his condo. I've got to play his game. Outsmart him if I can.* Amie was surprised when they drove past the ramp to the Route 90 Bridge, which led to Ocean City. *He's not taking me to his place.*

"Where are we going, Paul?" She swallowed hard.

"You'll see. You'll like it. Turn right onto Beauchamp Road and then drive into the entrance of the River Run Golf Course on your left."

She was very familiar with the River Run Golf Course and homes in that community. Her left hand shook as she flicked on the turn signal. *Have to stay calm. My heart won't stop racing.*

"Go all the way over to the country club." She did as she was told. Paul pointed. "See that empty space over there?" He pointed. "Pull into that spot." Amie took a deep breath, did as he said, and looked at Paul.

"Now what?" she asked.

"Take the keys out of the car and give them to me." Paul slipped them inside the pocket of his fisherman's shirt. "Now, get out of the car and walk in front of me toward the clubhouse, and remember I have a gun pointed at you."

"What are we going to do? Play twilight golf?" said Amie.

"I see you still haven't lost your sense of humor, Amie. Keep walking."

When they passed the entrance to the country club's restaurant, Paul said, "Walk down that path through that wooded area until you get to the pier."

Amie watched Paul look at his digital watch. It wouldn't be dark soon, and she was hoping she'd see someone.

Amie began walking on the dirt path, her legs still trembling. She reached into the left pocket of her jacket for her lipstick mace spray.

"Stop right there. What did you just pull out of your pocket? What's that in your hand? Drop it now," he said.

Amie's eyes welled up. She dropped her lipstick mace spray on the path. Paul picked it up. He realized what it was. Clasping it in his hand, he said, "You were going to spray me with this, weren't you?"

Tears rolled down her cheeks. He put the spray in his shirt pocket along with her keys.

"Of course you knew I was. You stole my pepper spray keychain from my bureau," she said.

Paul ignored her. "Walk onto the pier until you get to the end," he said.

He's going to drown me in the river. "Why are you wearing those heavy boots? Are you going to kill me? Is that your plan?

Are you going to drown me in this murky water?" Amie asked. Her heart was pounding too fast.

"Untie the two boat lines," Paul said. "Throw the lines inside the boat." She was acutely mindful that he was still pointing his gun at her. His boat was spacious, and Amie found it easy to board the full-length swim deck.

"Sit over there." He pointed to a cushioned seat near the steering wheel, and Amie sat across from him.

Paul took Amie's keys out of his pocket and placed them on the console. He made himself comfortable behind the steering wheel and stuffed his Ray-Bans into his shirt pocket. Amie watched Paul rest his gun between his legs on his seat in front of the helm. He shifted into neutral and started the engine. He then moved the throttle into the forward position. Paul was shifting the gears smoothly and working the controls to avoid picking up too much speed.

Amie watched with alarm as he steered the boat toward the middle of the Saint Martin's River. It was a smooth and dry ride. "I didn't know you knew how to steer a boat," Amie said.

"You don't know a lot about me, Amie," he said.

He let the boat drift in the middle of the river, avoiding the use of the anchor. "I brought you out here because I want us to have a private talk. You have been avoiding me. I don't understand why you want nothing to do with me. I'm not going to hurt you, Amie. I just want you to know how I feel about you. That's why we're out here in the river. Don't you feel something for me?"

Be smart. He's sick. Outwit him. Amie put her head down and said, "I thought you hated me because of your texts and emails. You hurt me very much by what you said." *Act. Be convincing. He has a gun.*

"Amie, I want you to know that I still love you more than you know, and I just want to find out if we have a chance to get back together. You heard me in court, didn't you? You have to believe me."

"It was hard for me to believe you. You scared me because you broke into my house, and you have me here by force because you pointed a gun at me, making me feel you were going to kill me."

"I'd never do that. You belong with me. I'd treat you so well if you were with me. I have money from my mother's estate. We could travel."

"Where could we go?" asked Amie.

"Anywhere you like. Greece. Spain. Paris."

Amie forced a smile. "It sounds too good. After I saw you, I found myself thinking about you. I even dreamed we were together, but I care about Patrick too."

"Do you really love that man you're married to? I don't think much of him at all. My mother loved you like a daughter. We could have lived in her house, and we would have been well off. You know that little house I bought?" Paul didn't wait for Amie to reply. "I wanted us to live there. I was going to rebuild and live in a huge, beautiful home on that property with you. It would have been so private. Just you and me. I thought so much of you that I even named you in my will as a beneficiary, leaving you most of everything I have. Your so-called husband can't take care of you and give you the things you want on his salary."

"Oh Paul, I didn't know. I'm dumbstruck you put me in your will. I did care a lot for you, but I felt back then that you didn't like some of things I enjoyed doing, like playing tennis, going to concerts, dancing, and things like that. I thought you weren't really happy with me. Patrick came along, and he liked a lot of the activities I liked to do."

"He's not good for you. I can make you very happy."

"What do you want me to do? Divorce him?"

"Why not, if you really care about me and want us to be together," Paul said. He smiled and winked at her.

Amie faked a smile. "Well, to tell you the truth, I haven't been real happy lately. He works late hours. Sometimes I think he's interested in someone else. I don't know. I could be wrong." *Hope he buys this bullshit.*

"See? I told you. You deserve better. That's usually a sign—-coming home very late at night. He says he's spying on a cheating husband, doesn't he?" Amie nodded. "He's probably seeing someone else. Don't you think about all the wives he sees of cheating husbands? Just because a cheating husband has an affair, doesn't mean his wife isn't an attractive woman. Patrick could have fallen for one of those good-looking wives. It happens. Think about leaving him, Amie."

Amie switched her position on the cushioned seat to get more comfortable. Her unzipped jacket opened, exposing her small pregnant belly. Paul's eyes grew wide as he saw her stomach revealed. His face became a dark red color, and the vein in the middle of his brow started to throb.

He raised his voice. "You're pregnant, aren't you? Why did you go and do that? I thought you said you weren't happy. I can't believe this." His nostrils widened, and his eyebrows pointed toward the middle of his forehead, making a V-shape. Teeth bared, he said, "Are you lying to me? Why would you want a baby with him if you said you weren't happy? How can we be together if you have that man's baby in your stomach? You should get rid of it." His eyes narrowed.

"I was—"

Paul started the engine and shoved the throttle forward, heading back toward the pier.

Amie's lip quivered, her eyes wide with fear. She held back tears and looked to see if any boats were coming their way. She spotted two boats in the distance, but they were too far away for her to be heard if she yelled out to them, and Paul's boat was picking up speed in the opposite direction. Amie placed her arms on the back rim, gripping the edge of the boat to keep her balance. Paul was going so fast, maybe thirty-five knots.

The kidney-jarring action of the boat was making Amie nauseous. Paul's gun slid to the floor beneath his seat. He backed off the throttle a bit when they got a little closer to the pier. Amie saw a boat come out from a cove across the way, still too far to call out. Paul's Hurricane boat jolted, and a grinding noise could be heard near the motor. Amie's keys fell off the console. She recovered from the joggling action of the boat and bent down to pick up her car keys.

The boat had become grounded in the shallow water. Seriously grounded. "Damn it!" said Paul. He revved the engine and stirred up the bottom, causing mud and sand to go into the engine.

"Shit. We're stuck in the sand." He stood up and walked to the stern and peered overboard to look down at the engine.

CHAPTER 24

Amie quickly rose out of her seat and snatched the gun off the floor and threw it into the river as far as she could. *He's not gonna use that on me.* The boat she saw in the distance came closer to Paul's Sun Deck Hurricane.

Amie saw her chance and yelled, "Help! We're stuck!" She waved her arms back and forth and jumped up and down. "Help!" she said again. They aimed their cabin cruiser in the direction of Paul's boat.

Paul raised his voice. "What are you doing?" Sweat dripped down his cheeks. "Stop yelling. Don't do that. Sit down." He looked over at the helm and then the floor. "Where's my gun?"

"What? I don't know," said Amie. The cabin cruiser came closer. Paul revved the engine again. Through her tears, Amie risked crying out for help again. Her screams were louder. Flapping her arms again, she cried out, "I have to get out of here! Help me! He's keeping me here against my will!" *Amie looked down into the water. It's shallow. I'm jumping out.* She hurried over to the bow and jumped into the river.

Amie's feet landed in the water up to her knees. The bottom felt mushy on the soles of her shoes. The cabin cruiser moved toward Paul's boat but did not get close. Its engine was turned off. Amie waded through the water toward the men in the cruiser. They secured the ladder over the edge, and she tried to climb up into the boat.

"Take your time," said the one man. "You're not in any danger." Amie glanced back and saw Paul head toward the shore on foot. The one man extended his arm for Amie to grasp, and they helped her into their boat.

"That guy knows nothing about the depths of this river," the one boatman said.

She turned to the two in the boat and said, "You rescued me from a dangerous man who forced me into his boat. He had a gun, but I grabbed it and threw it into the water. I'm in debt to both of you. Thank you so much. Can you please call the police?"

"I already called the Coast Guard, ma'am," said boatman number two.

Their cabin cruiser sped away from the pier. Amie was seated near the stern, the wind ruffling her hair. She watched Paul in the distance as the waves beat against the rickety pier.

"The Coast Guard's pretty far away, aren't they?" Amie asked.

"Their small-boat station is located near the southernmost tip of the Ocean City peninsula. It shouldn't take long before they get here," said boatman number one. "They have a variety of boats...a twenty-four-foot low-draft boat that maneuvers across the shifting sandbars where the water depth can drastically change from a few feet to a depth of only mere inches should be what they'll use."

"How do you know all this?" asked Amie.

"I used to work at that boat station."

Patrick was worried sick. It was past 5:30 p.m., and Amie wasn't home yet. He dialed her cell phone number. Her line buzzed repeatedly and went to voice mail. *Odd. I know it's her last day teaching for a while, but she knows we're going out for dinner.* He called her again, pacing the tiled floor in the kitchen. When she didn't answer, he bolted to the front door, knocking over a tall glass of ice tea on top of the kitchen counter.

Driving along Ocean Parkway, Patrick watched every car as they passed him on the other side of the road, thinking he'd see Amie's car. He pulled into the community center's parking lot and drove around searching for Amie's Mini Cooper. It wasn't there. As he turned down the row to go back home, his head turned to the left, and his eyes spotted her red duffel bag on the parking lot beside a car. He got out of his Seville and retrieved the bag. Patrick unzipped it and saw that her phone was inside.

After another thirty minutes, with no word from Amie, he called the police. He explained how she was being stalked by Paul. "Look at the reports she filed."

They told him she couldn't be considered a missing person yet, which he had expected. He then called Crabbe.

After seeing the damage, Paul knew full well it would be impossible for him to get his Hurricane out of the sand. He thought he had a good knowledge of the river's depths. Apparently not. Paul had not been aware of the shifting sandbars, and he hadn't been watching the depth finder gauge on his console. Too busy thinking about Amie. He was shocked to learn that she was pregnant. It complicated everything.

He was distraught over his Hurricane SunDeck being stuck aground. He loved that boat, and his plan to keep Amie with him had failed. Paul remembered she had said she was unhappy. *I didn't realize she really does care for me.*

He actually believed she had feelings for him. After listening to her, he felt he had a chance to win her back. But why did Amie have to get pregnant? It infuriated him. *Maybe it was an accident. Happens all the time.*

When she cried out for help to the other boat, Paul became panic stricken. He saw the cabin cruiser heading toward his Hurricane and quickly decided to jump into the river and head to the pier near the golf course. Paul made his way in less-than-knee-deep water toward the shore. He trudged through the marsh and tall grasses, not worried he'd get bit by another copperhead. His sturdy boots protected him from that. When he made it to shore, he hastened his steps while passing the driving range. His right hand searched his pocket, feeling only the mace spay.

"Damn it," he said. "I left Amie's car keys on the console." He shook his head. "Can't drive away in her car."

At the end of the dirt trail was the cart path to the first hole running along the right side of the clubhouse. He turned left off the dusty trail and walked on the cart path toward the first hole. Four golfers had started their game on the back nine and proceeded in their carts to play the front nine, passing Paul on his right.

Paul heard their voices near the first hole. He hid behind a spruce tree watching the four golfers on the first tee box. He saw one of the men take a practice swing before hitting his drive on the par-four hole. The other three golfers fell silent.

Paul crept quietly over to the golf cart on the path while the men's backs were toward him. He hopped into the cart, turned the key in the ignition, and drove down the cart path.

Just as one of the golfers was about to tee off, his partner began shouting.

"Hey, what are you doing? That's our golf cart!" "Come back here, asshole!"

"What the fuck? He's got our clubs."

"And my cell phone," the one golfer said.

His golf partner called the pro shop and explained what had just happened. The pro said, "I'll call the police, and I'll come down there to help you catch him." The pro instructor ran over to the golf shed that housed the carts and grabbed one. He drove toward the first hole and followed two of the golfers in their cart after Paul. The two remaining golfers ran back to the shed and got a golf cart to join the chase.

Paul had already driven his cart over a small wooden bridge to the second hole, which was a par three. He glanced behind him and didn't see or hear the golfers who were on the first hole. He kept driving his cart, passing a porta potty. *Gotta pee but can't stop here.* Paul continued down the cart path, passing the par-five third hole. *Can't this thing go faster? It's not even hitting fifteen miles per hour. Shit.*

Paul read his watch. It was close to 7:30 p.m. It would be dark in an hour. He rounded the bend of the path and came upon another par-three hole. A single male golfer had just finished hitting across a large pond and onto the green. He was putting his club back into his bag when Paul skirted around him on the cart path. Paul said "Hi" as he drove past him and saw the puzzled look on the golfer's face. Paul continued forward to the par-five fifth hole, not realizing yet that three carts were a distance behind, chasing after him.

When Paul rounded the curve away from the green and the pond, he was on the other side of the par-three hole. He glanced across the pond, and he saw men in three carts on the same path he had been traveling, advancing in his direction aiming to catch up to him. Paul drove farther down the cart path of the par-five hole. The fifth hole ran along Beauchamp Road. Paul saw his chance to ditch the cart and conceal it behind a cluster of tall pine trees along the right side of the path. He watched as a police car raced by on Beauchamp Road heading toward the entrance to the golf course. On the other side of the road, a line of trees bordered Beauchamp Road almost all the way up to Racetrack Road. Behind the trees, backyards of houses in Ocean Pines extended up to the main road also.

Paul hid the cart well behind the huge pines. He saw a cell phone in the opening behind the steering wheel in the golf cart and grabbed it before stepping out of the cart. "Might need this."

Paul then darted across the road to the backyard of one of the houses in Ocean Pines. He hurried over to a shed and stayed behind it. It wasn't long before the pursuers in the three carts across the road drove by on the cart path heading toward the sixth hole. They missed seeing the golf cart that Paul had masked behind the large trees. He laughed as they continued on their hunt.

Paul took a leak at the side of the shed and zipped up his pants. He was familiar with the area and planned to head toward his old house. He ran across Beauchamp Road and sprinted to a church parking lot. He eyed another police car traveling on Racetrack Road and hid behind a dumpster in back of the church. He wiped the perspiration off his brow. *That was close.* He began running in the opposite direction when the police car turned onto Beauchamp Road. He dashed across the parking lot of a private school beyond the church and headed into the woods. He stopped to catch his breath, resting the palms of this hands on his knees. Paul knew exactly where he was. The woods would empty out onto the winding road up to his old, little house. He was camouflaged well in the woods and stomped unafraid farther along in his boots to his destination. He walked about three hundred yards.

There it is—the tunnel of trees and the narrow road to my old house. What a beautiful sight.

Thoroughly spent, Paul stumbled and tripped, stubbing his toe on a rock lying on the dirt path, and he fell forward, losing his balance. He got up and trudged to his former house.

CHAPTER 25

Behind the small house was the mammoth framework of the Dillons' country house. Paul saw that the frame of their house was made from light structural lumber from pine and fir trees. He inhaled. *The freshly cut wood really smells good.* The floor joints were made from south yellow pines. Their construction team had done a great framing job.

The Dillons should love their new home when it's all completed. This could have been mine and Amie's.

Paul inspected the area behind the unfinished house. The Dillons had cleared away a lot of trees, shrubs, and bushes.

Must have cost a bundle.

Many logs were scattered around. Paul saw holes in the ground and random materials spread everywhere on the construction site. There was equipment for lifting heavy loads. Beams, hazard tape, and ladders as well as hand and power tools were lying on the ground and inside the framed house. Paul walked past a cement mixer, wheelbarrow, and a pile of bricks. He was totally tired but wanted to see more. The shed and shanty were still standing.

He went around to the front of his old house. He exhaled noisily. *I'm beat.* He pushed open the screen door of the porch. Only ripped screening remained. The home's front door was taken off its hinges. His brand-new carpet had been removed. In the living room, the rattan chair was missing, as well as the walnut kitchen table. The one leather chair remained. He noticed there was no glass in the windows. He walked over to the kitchen sink. *So thirsty.* No water poured out of the faucet. *Must have turned the water off.* In the bathroom, Paul saw that the tub was gone. He walked a little farther and saw that his double-size bed was still there. Sighing at the comforting sight of his bed, and being so physically drained, he collapsed in an exhausted heap on top of the mattress and immediately fell into a sound sleep.

⚓

Patrick received a call from Amie. "Where are you? I've been out of my mind with worry."

"This is the first chance I had to call you. I didn't have my phone. I'm with the police at the Coast Guard station number 146," said Amie.

"What? Are you OK?"

"Yes, I am now, thank goodness."

"I have your phone and duffel bag," said Patrick.

Amie explained the whole story to Patrick, from the time she left the community center up to the time she was rescued by the two boatmen. She explained to Patrick that they eventually met up with the Ocean City Coast Guard.

"I switched over to the Coast Guard's low-draft boat after one of the boatmen contacted them. We headed to where the

SunDeck was run aground. The Coast Guardsmen contacted a towing service. I pointed to where the gun was tossed into the water."

"What? The gun?" said Patrick. "Paul had a gun?"

"Yes. He used the gun to force me into my car and drive to the marina where his boat was. I managed to throw the gun in the water when the boat got stuck in the sand. The Coast Guard searched in the shallow water and were able to retrieve it. While they were there, a towboat arrived, and the men worked on getting Paul's wedged boat out of the sand. The towboat had a squared-off bow and a hull that was flat-bottomed for the shallow waters. It was a tough job, and they almost gave up, thinking they would wait for a higher tide so that the boat could float off. The tow guy mentioned he hoped the owner of the SunDeck boat had towing insurance and noticed that there was damage to the engine. We cruised back to the station after they were done with the job. So much for my action-packed day on the water."

"Did he know you were pregnant?"

"Yes."

"That son of a bitch. I could kill him," said Patrick.

"It's over, Patrick. There's something else. You'll never guess what Paul said to me," said Amie.

"What? I know he probably told you how much he wanted to be with you and how much he thought I was a loser and couldn't provide well for you," said Patrick.

"Yes, he said all that, but you won't believe this, but he said that he was leaving me most of his estate in his will. According to him, he was pretty wealthy."

"Really? You believed him? That's probably a crock, Amie," said Patrick.

"Well, his mother was very well off. I know that much, and she probably left everything in her will to Paul," said Amie.

"Maybe, but he lived in a one-bedroom apartment. And then, why did he buy that awful shack in the woods? And didn't he tell you he could afford anything when he wanted you to show him houses in Ocean Pines? Didn't seem like he had a lot of money if he rented a condo in Ocean City. Amie, I don't want to waste another minute talking. I'm coming to get you. Do you need me to bring you anything?"

"No, I just want you," Amie said.

At the crack of dawn, the Ocean Pines Police Department, Patrick, Hulk, and Crabbe organized a search party to try to find Paul. Hulk assigned four detectives to scour the Ocean City area. He raised his voice and urged the detectives, "Find this guy as expediently as possible." He then assigned two detectives to travel over the Route 90 Bridge to Ocean City to see if Paul was at his condo first.

"Let's get this asshole," said Hulk.

Patrick contacted Chip Hammond and asked for his assistance. Chip made plans to call a couple of Paul's acquaintances to learn if they knew where he could be hiding. Crabbe's assignment was to join the detectives to search along the beaches and shorelines with the K-9 dogs. Patrick headed to Ocean Pines and the wooded areas along Assawoman Bay and the Saint Martin's River.

Chip met with Paul's friend Tim, who was floored when he heard what had happened.

"I have no clue where he is. Did you check his condo?" Handing Chip a Post-it note with Kim's phone number, Tim said, "You might want to talk to Kim Archer, his girlfriend. I find this hard to believe about him. He's a great guy."

Chip said he thought the police were checking Paul's unit, but he would call Kim. Tim gave him the names of some of the hang-outs or bars that Paul and he frequented. Chip dialed Kim's number and identified himself as well as describing why he was asking about Paul's whereabouts.

"No way. I don't believe he did that. And he was on probation? And he has a restraining order against him? What a jerk. We're not together anymore. I have no idea where he could be hiding out. He's so weird. I'm so happy now that I broke up with him," Kim said.

After speaking with Kim and getting nowhere, Chip proceeded to visit his brief list of bars where Paul and Tim hung out. Maybe he would uncover some revealing clue about Paul from questioning the bartenders.

Within a short period of time, the media got wind of the grounded boat, the abduction and rescue of Amie McCombe, the abductor, Paul Simmons, and the search party. WBOC-TV, the Wave, and other TV and radio stations were buzzing with the breaking news.

More detectives from Salisbury and surrounding areas joined the search for Paul—a search that included combing outlets, the River Run Golf Course, the Ocean Pines community, Ocean City malls, Salisbury neighborhoods, and wooded areas. The police pursuit also involved sweeps by two helicopters across the Delmarva area.

Later, after Patrick dropped Amie off at Cici's and Joe's house, Amie attentively watched the noon news on WBOC-TV with Cici.

"We have breaking news from Berlin, Maryland. A female Ocean Pines resident was rescued by the Coast Guard on the Saint Martin's River. She had been abducted. The suspect, age thirty-nine, Paul Simmons, is at large. If you have any information on his whereabouts, please call the Ocean Pines Police Department immediately at 410-524-5555."

"That was a good photo of him, but the TV reporter failed to mention the two men who were responsible for really saving me. I'll call the TV station to see if they would acknowledge them," Amie said. "I really would like to do something for those two boatmen, like maybe treat them to dinner."

"You were so lucky not to be injured. You had to be terrified for your life," said Cici.

"I was so frightened. Scared out of a year's growth. If I hadn't jumped out of that boat when I did...I shudder to think about what could have happened to me and my baby."

"But this time, when they catch him, he'll be put away for good," said Cici.

CHAPTER 26

In the bedroom early that morning, Paul was in a deep sleep, blocking the outside world. He didn't hear the clamor outside the house. He slept through contractors putting up temporary fencing around the small house. Ari Dillon, Susan Dillon, and Kyle, their contractor, watched as the men worked.

The hydraulic excavator rammed into the side of the house. It weakened and buckled the supports of the central floors, and the top part of the house collapsed onto the bottom. The roof came down. All of the aluminum siding toppled. The studs supporting the walls were undermined. The windows caved in. The bulldozer on the other side plowed into the front porch and crushed its rotting wood. Fire hoses were used to control the dust the demolition created. The small house was no more. The area where it had stood was completely leveled— a complete teardown. It was over in seconds.

Ari and Susan wore white painters' masks over their noses as they watched. When the dust diminished, they removed their masks. Flecks of dust and particles covered their jackets.

"This is amazing," said Ari.

"What a mess it creates, though," said Susan, shaking her head.

"See those skid loaders over there?" he said as he pointed. "They'll haul the debris off to a twenty-yard dumpster."

"I'm glad we saved some things for reuse and recycling, like the hardware and metal fixtures. The knobs and tub are certainly reusable," Susan said.

"The whole hauling process will take anywhere from a day to a week or more, and then we can decide where Kyle can build the animal pens and cages."

"Let's go back home and let them finish their job," Susan said.

⊨

Hulk called off the search party and informed Amie. "We've searched everywhere. He's gone. He could have hopped a plane to Belize in Central America for all we know."

"I'll still worry he's right around the corner," Amie said.

"Well, he can't be anywhere near here," Hulk said. "We've combed the areas from Rehoboth Beach to Salisbury. He's not around here."

Amie sat at her desk. *He'll come back. I just feel it. He'll come back and get me.*

Amie's phone buzzed while she was at a meeting with the other realtors in the conference room. She didn't recognize the number and decided to call the unknown caller back after her meeting. Her coworkers adjourned the meeting and decided to go to lunch at Taylor's, and Amie felt less relaxed now that the search party was canceled. She tried to enjoy herself at lunch with her colleagues.

She and the others left Taylor's, and Amie headed back to her office. When she sat at her desk, she checked her voice mail. She learned that the unknown caller was Patrick's secretary. She had left a message that said, "Mrs. McCombe, this is Mary Olson—you know, Patrick's new secretary at his office. Please call me at your earliest convenience." Amie was mad at herself for not calling her right back before lunch. She dialed her cell phone number.

"Hi, Mary. Sorry I didn't return your call sooner. What's up?"

"Patrick just left the office to go to Paul Simmons's old house, and he told me to call you. It seems that the new owners of that old house found some personal items on the path leading up to their property that might be connected to the case. Since information about the search for Simmons was all over the news and the owners of that property knew that Simmons abducted you, they called Chief Phillips. They thought maybe their findings could be of value to the police," said Mary.

Amie hung up. *Paul's still here.*

Hulk, Joe, Patrick, and several detectives from the Ocean Pines Police Department were at the scene of the Dillons' property. Ari and Susan gathered with the detectives and Hulk.

"Do you think Paul Simmons is hiding in the woods around here?" Ari asked.

"It looks like he was here. That lipstick spray you found belongs to Patrick McCombe's wife," said Hulk.

"Susan spotted men's sunglasses and mace spray in the middle of the road up to our property when we walked to our car to go back to Salisbury," said Ari.

"Thank you for contacting Chief Phillips. You had no idea it was truly connected to the case." said Patrick.

"We can't believe Mr. Simmons abducted your wife. He seems like such a nice man," said Susan.

Patrick took a deep breath, forcing himself to stay calm. "We're going to search your property and the surrounding area," he said.

"When did they complete the demolition of the house?" asked Patrick.

"This morning. You'd be surprised how fast it took to crumble it to pieces," said Ari. Patrick squinted at the dismantled house and looked around the property with his hands on his hips.

"Did you clear out everything you could beforehand?" asked Patrick.

"Yes, we looked at salvageable and recycled items to donate. We worked with the contractor to help us recover things that could be resold or donated prior to tearing down the house."

"Did you do a preinspection before the house was demolished?" asked Patrick.

"Absolutely. Twice, in fact. After the construction crew knocked off yesterday at 5:00 p.m., the demolition project manager said that we were good to go. Why?" asked Ari.

"Just trying to cover all the bases," said Patrick.

The men searched on foot around the property and in the woods and down to the river. The construction crew halted their project until the next day.

Early the next morning, the crew set to work removing the debris. The men worked hard loading the remnants. The haulers planned to move the debris to an approved dump site and dispose of it. Some of the things the haulers needed to get rid of were the disturbed trees and bushes, rocks, bricks, dirt, lumber, rubble resulting from construction, rags, bottles, metal scrap shavings, weeds, and solid waste. A lot of stuff.

They weren't prepared for what they found under the collapsed roof.

"Is that what I think it is?" one of the crew members asked.

The men gathered around the crushed body. "What the hell?"

A couple of the men scurried away from their discovery. "Get the foreman." The crew left the scene and assembled away from the demolished house near the loader and waited for their boss. It was a gruesome picture. The foreman, after seeing the body's condition, dashed over to the woods and barfed. Not a pretty sight.

The police secured the area around the demolition site with yellow crime-scene barrier tape. Hulk didn't want any nosy people snooping around the site, and he wanted to wait for an official cause of death from the coroner. Hulk, Crabbe, and Patrick felt it undoubtedly was Paul's body. They waited for the coroner to remove the remains. They left to go to their respective offices after the horrible discovery. "The coroner has his work cut out for him," said Hulk.

They drove away separately in their cars. Patrick looked back at the wretched scene in his rearview mirror. *I'm glad he's dead.*

CHAPTER 27

The Dillons headed back to the construction site two days later. They ventured up the driveway in their SUV to the dismal spot and walked the rest of the way to their property, eyeing the yellow tape. They scanned the area, and both looked so forlorn. "I'm heartbroken this happened," said Ari.

"I know, dear. Me too."

"They should be removing that tape soon. As soon as they do, the hauling crew should be coming back to remove more junk."

"I'll call the police department and ask when they can remove it, now that the body is gone," said Susan.

"So horrific a thing," said Ari. "His head was struck by some firm object and was buried under the fallen material. Imagine having a heavy roof come collapsing down on top of you."

"It's a terrible shame. He probably didn't know what hit him. Are you sure our insurance guy said we won't get sued?"

"I'm sure, Susan. The house was given a demolition inspection the day before. We had a No Trespassing sign put up outside the house by the crew's supervisor. And Simmons was running from the police and looking for a good place to hide out after committing a crime. We didn't hide him. He shouldn't have been around a construction site in the first place. It's hazardous. Accidents happen. It's all on the demolition crew. They're supposed to follow specific safety practices before destroying a house. That's not our job. Stop worrying."

They strolled over to the construction of their new house. "I can't wait until it's finished," Susan said.

While they assessed their contractor's work, they jotted down questions for him to answer. They were too busy to notice what was occurring in the area behind them. From out of the tangled rubble, it moved smoothly, wriggling on the ground with its yellow tail tip and hourglass-shaped crossbands prominently in view. The three-foot long copperhead slithered into the woods toward its home near the river.

⚔

Amie picked at the scrambled egg on her plate. Patrick said, "Aren't you hungry, Amie? You look like you're deep in thought. Something wrong?"

Amie glanced up at Patrick and said, "Patrick, please don't get mad at me, but I have to ask—"

Patrick interrupted her. "Ask what?"

"Please don't get upset with me," she said. "But that day all of you were searching for Paul, everyone split up to search in different areas, right?"

"Yeah," said Patrick.

"Was Joe with you when you were looking for Paul?"

"No," said Patrick. "I searched the Ocean Pines area and the woods. Joe combed the shoreline. Why?"

Amie asked, "Did you happen to go back to Paul's old shack that day?"

"No, I didn't," said Patrick. "I went everywhere but not there. Where are you going with this, Amie?"

"I just thought maybe you might have gone back to Paul's old house and maybe found him and got into a fight with him. Maybe you—"

"You think I went back there, discovered he was there, and what...and beat him to death?"

"Well...yeah. I was thinking maybe you went back there. Maybe you didn't want to tell me and kept it a secret. Maybe if you two had gotten into a terrible fight and Paul died, it all happened in self-defense."

Patrick's mouth slightly opened, his eyes almost closed, and his head tilted to one side. He gave a small shake of his head. He looked at her in disbelief. "What you're saying is--did I kill Paul? That's incredulous."

Amie was speechless. She looked at him, tears blurring her eyes.

"Amie, answer me. You think I murdered him and left him in that house? I can't believe this."

"Patrick, I know you were in the area. I know you were obsessed with catching him. I know that you stayed in Paul's shack back when you were waiting to arrest him when he violated his probation. Now please don't be upset with me. Remember you went to his apartment in Salisbury that one day and had heated words with him? You were boiling mad. You kept it from me. You said you wanted to pummel him. You said you could kill him when you learned he held a gun on me. Your exact words."

"Amie, I didn't kill him. I didn't go to his place. Maybe I should have. Maybe I could have prevented what happened to him before they demolished the house. I didn't do it."

"I just had to ask. I'm sorry. Patrick. I know you've always wanted to protect me from him. You insinuated he could kill me, and you were right. I think he would have, especially after he found out we were going to have a baby. I love you so much. Please forgive me," said Amie, sniffing. "This past year has been such a tough ordeal. I'm not thinking clearly. Paul was so off balance. I didn't mean to upset you."

"Amie, the coroner's autopsy concluded that he was struck in the head with a heavy object when everything came crashing down on top of him." Patrick put his hands on his hips. "I had nothing to do with his death. The house caving down on him killed him, and he probably suffocated. I can't believe you'd think that I'm capable of doing something like that."

She put her arms around him and buried her head in his chest. "I believe you."

He shook his head. "I hope you do, Amie. But just for the record, I'm really glad he's gone." Patrick shoved his chair away from the kitchen table and immediately left the room.

Amie ran after him. "Don't leave like this. Don't be mad at me," she said.

Patrick sighed, stopped in his tracks, and turned around to look at her.

Amie wrapped her arms around him. "Forgive me, please. I don't doubt you, Patrick."

"OK. OK. I forgive you."

"Patrick, I need to tell you something else."

"Now what?" he asked.

Amie sat down on the sofa. "Come here. Sit down." She patted the sofa's cushion. "After Paul's body was discovered and you and Joe went to the morgue, I saw my OB/GYN for an ultrasound. I wanted to make sure everything was all right with the baby after being on the boat with Paul."

Patrick's brow furrowed. He took a deep breath. "Are you and the baby OK?"

"Yes," she said, patting his knee. She smiled. "I know the sex of the baby."

"You do?" asked Patrick.

"Do you want to know?"

"Yes, of course I do," said Patrick.

"We're having a baby girl," Amie told him.

Amie and Cici walked down to the end of her pier. They sat down on the wooden planks and let their legs dangle over its edge. It was still a warm-like summer afternoon for the end of September even though it was officially fall after September 22.

"How are you really doing?" asked Cici.

"I'm fine, actually." Amie told her about the ultrasound and what it revealed.

"Wow. That's the best news," said Cici. "I'm so happy for you."

"Also, Paul's lawyer, Jim Reynolds, called me earlier. He said that Paul left me quite a bit of money from his estate."

"He had money? I didn't know he was well off," said Cici.

"Apparently his mother left him a handsome inheritance, and Paul had saved a lot. But I don't know if I want it."

Cici said, "You shouldn't turn it down after all you've been through. Put it in a trust for your daughter."

"It doesn't feel right," Amie said.

"I'd accept it if it were me," said Cici. "I had no qualms taking all of Greg's assets after what happened to him."

"Patrick told me that Paul was a loner. No one had a memorial service for him. Patrick knew of one friend he had in Salisbury, and of course, Paul was friendly with his probation officer. I don't remember Paul having any family members other than his mother," said Amie.

Cici said, "He would want you to have it. Put it to good use. It seems he didn't have any beneficiaries except you. He was a lone wolf."

"Well, maybe you're correct. I could give a large donation to Susan Dillon's animal rescue farm and start a college fund for Rayne."

"Rayne? You're naming your daughter Rayne?" Cici asked.

"Yes. You didn't claim it, and I really liked the name when you suggested it for your baby."

Cici laughed. "Lindsay and Rayne will be great friends. The people in our lives." Cici shook her head. "On one hand, we'll have two wonderful girls. However, on the other hand, we had two real dirtbags for men…Greg and Paul…didn't we?" Cici shook her head. "They were so rotten to us. We don't have to worry about men losers in our lives anymore. Right, Amie? Amie?" Cici nudged her shoulder.

After a prolonged pause, Amie turned her gaze away from the horizon to Cici's face. She looked intently and steadily at Cici, holding her eyes for several seconds, and said, "Cici, I hope you're right. God, I pray you're right. We'll see."

ACKNOWLEDGEMENTS

Pursuit in Ocean Pines is a work of fiction. Names, characters, events, and incidents are used in a fictitious manner. Any similarity to real life is purely coincidental.

I would like to thank everyone in developing this novel.

Special thanks goes to the editors at Palmetto Publishing Group. Very helpful was *OC Today* and Tom Neale's articles in *Boat US*, and I appreciate the information given about the DMV from Rob Adams and Mike Lynch. Thanks also goes to Kathleen Baty, advocate for women who have been stalked. Thank you, Vicki, for sharing your story, Sandy Bartkowiak for your contribution, and Jamie Tucker.

And I cannot forget the immeasurable support given to me by Tom, Holly, and Casey.

ABOUT THE AUTHOR

Dana Phipps lives in Maryland and spends her summers with her family in Ocean Pines. Wanting to continue with the same characters in her first novel, *Murder in Ocean Pines*, *Pursuit in Ocean Pines* became the sequel. She wrote two children's books, *Emily and Hurricane Isabel* and *Emily and Her Pouting Puffer Fish*, before writing her first novel.

CPSIA information can be obtained
at www.ICGtesting.com
Printed in the USA
LVHW021728120819
627349LV00013B/1222/P

9 781641 114011